Fortune Telling . . .

"Come on, Gypsy woman, read my fortune." It was both a dare and a taunt.

With an unsteady forefinger, Shea touched his long, evenly balanced thumb. "Theories, problems, working out solutions, unraveling mysteries—those are the things you do best. You perceive nature as something to be understood and utilized." Where were the words coming from?

"How much did they tell you?" Dave demanded.

"If you mean your sister Jean, she said you had the disposition of an injured warthog."

"That much you could see for yourself," he muttered, not satisfied the two of them hadn't set him up.

"According to your thumb, you have an enormous store of emotional energy, you're as stubborn as a drunken mule, ████████████████████ ██ companion." S████████████████████ vere married once, ████████████████████ r relationship, a██████████

Dear Reader:

SILHOUETTE DESIRE is an exciting new line of contemporary romances from Silhouette Books. During the past year, many Silhouette readers have written in telling us what other types of stories they'd like to read from Silhouette, and we've kept these comments and suggestions in mind in developing SILHOUETTE DESIRE.

DESIREs feature all of the elements you like to see in a romance, plus a more sensual, provocative story. So if you want to experience all the excitement, passion and joy of falling in love, then SILHOUETTE DESIRE is for you.

For more details write to:

Jane Nicholls
Silhouette Books
PO Box 236
Thornton Road
Croydon
Surrey CR9 3RU

DIXIE BROWNING
In the Palm of Her Hand

Silhouette Desire

Originally Published by Silhouette Books
division of
Harlequin Enterprises Ltd.

All the characters in this book have no existence outside the imagination of the Author, and have no relation whatsoever to anyone bearing the same name or names. They are not even distantly inspired by any individual known or unknown to the Author, and all the incidents are pure invention.

The text of this publication or any part thereof may not be reproduced or transmitted in any form or by any means, electronic or mechanical, including photocopying, recording, storage in an information retrieval system, or otherwise, without the written permission of the publisher.

This book is sold subject to the condition that it shall not, by way of trade or otherwise, be lent, resold, hired out or otherwise circulated without the prior consent of the publisher in any form of binding or cover other than that in which it is published and without a similar condition including this condition being imposed on the subsequent purchaser.

*First published in Great Britain 1986
by Silhouette Books, 15–16 Brook's Mews, London W1A 1DR*

© Dixie Browning 1986

Silhouette, Silhouette Desire and Colophon are Trade Marks
of Harlequin Enterprises B.V.

ISBN 0 373 50400 4

22–0786

*Printed and bound in Great Britain by
Cox & Wyman Ltd, Reading*

DIXIE BROWNING

is a native of North Carolina. When she isn't traveling to research her books, she divides her time between her home in Winston-Salem and her cottage at Buxton on Hatteras Island.

Other Silhouette Books by Dixie Browning

Silhouette Special Edition

Finders Keepers
Reach Out to Cherish
Just Desserts
Time and Tide
By Any Other Name

Silhouette Desire

Shadow of Yesterday
Image of Love
The Hawk and the Honey
Late Rising Moon
Stormwatch
The Tender Barbarian
Matchmaker's Moon
A Bird in Hand

For further information about
Silhouette Books please write to:

Jane Nicholls
Silhouette Books
PO Box 236
Thornton Road
Croydon
Surrey CR9 3RU

To Isabel Swift, whose insight and expertise
has enabled me to be me.

One

Shea thrust open the door of the taxi and flinched as a flurry of cold rain stung her face. It had taken her five days to get this far. Five days of flying and being airsick; of waiting in crowded terminals for a last-minute cancellation; of rushing to equally crowded bus stations when none materialized, struggling with her two huge, heavy bags, worrying about losing her stockpile of silver and all her tools if she left them unattended for a single moment. She'd never been so tired in all her life.

"You will wait for me, won't you?" she asked anxiously, leaning her head back inside.

"Lady, I ain't been paid yet," the driver said pointedly as he slid down in the seat and pulled his cap over his eyes.

Tugging her thin yellow raincoat more closely around her, Shea ducked her head, strode through a puddle, swore softly and ran for shelter, dodging the untrimmed branches of camellia and azalea bushes that whipped her legs from both sides of the mossy brick walkway. She was reaching for the tarnished door knocker, when the door was thrust open and a harried-looking woman burst out. She jumped back just in time to keep from being run over.

"Oh, m'gosh, did I scare you? Sorry, just trying to get to the post office before it closes." The woman glanced at a Mickey Mouse watch and grimaced. "Never make it. Drat!"

Shea crossed her arms and clasped her shoulders in an effort to stave off the cold. Could this be the wife of the man she'd come so far to see? Somewhere in her late forties, the woman was attractive enough, in spite of a liberal covering of animal hairs on the heavy mackinaw she wore over baggy flannel slacks.

Shea envied her the clothes. She hadn't bothered to buy anything yet, as she had no idea where she'd be going once this odyssey was ended. Clothes that were suitable for tropical Chiapas didn't quite fill the bill for a North Carolina winter. "Is your—ah . . ."

"Look, come on inside before you freeze to death. Heat's off everywhere but the kitchen, but at least we can get out of this wind."

Shea turned uncertainly toward the cab, and the older woman followed her glance. "If you want to let him go, I'll be glad to give you a lift wherever you're going. But that's a Wilmington cab, isn't it?"

Shea nodded, shivering as a rainy gust flung back the edge of her coat. She'd flown into Wilmington, the nearest airport, and taken a taxi for the last leg of her journey. She was still no closer to chosing a place to settle down permanently than she'd been when she'd left Mexico. "I hadn't thought that far, actually. I—ah, just came to deliver a letter to your husband."

"A letter for Pete? How come you brought it out here?"

"Pete?" Granddad had called him "Dave." Shea herself had thought of him as "Kilo Alpha" since the first time she'd heard the deep, distinctive drawl identifying him with the call letters assigned each amateur radio operator by the FCC.

She frowned. Her frown was interrupted by a sneeze. "David Pendleton? Isn't this where he lives?"

"Dave?" The woman emitted a snort of laughter. "Oh, I thought you said my husband. Dave's my brother. I'm Jean Cummings, by the way. Do I look like the sort of woman Dave would hook up with voluntarily?"

Completely at sea, Shea could only stare. Brother, husband—what difference did it make? All she wanted to do was to deliver the letter and find some quiet, safe place to collapse. "I'm Shea Bellwood. My grandfather—my late grandfather, that is—was a friend of your brother's. Edward Bellwood?" she prompted, as if the name itself might explain everything. "My grandfather was a ham operator, too. Ham radio. He and KA4—your brother, I mean—had a regular schedule. They used to talk once or twice a week, depending on propagation."

"Depending on *who*?"

"Skip, skip—the band. Reception!" She explained a little desperately, reaching for the terms she'd heard her grandfather use to explain the atmospheric conditions that governed radio reception.

Jean Cummings was looking at her as though she'd lapsed into gibberish. Perhaps she had, Shea thought tiredly. "Look, all I know is that before he died, Granddad made me promise that when I came back to the States I'd deliver this letter to KA4ZDE."

"This KA person is my brother David, I presume."

Shea nodded. If she needed further evidence that she'd embarked on a crazy mission, it took only trying to explain it to someone else. She felt like a refugee from a spy movie. All she needed was a trench coat and a pair of dark glasses.

"Okay, I'm with you this far, at least. They're both ham operators, right? And you've got something your grandfather was sending to Dave." Jean tilted her head, causing her graying ponytail to swing wildly. "Hey, did you say 'back to the States'? Where've you been, anyway, if you don't mind my asking?"

"For the past eleven years I lived in Mexico with my grandfather. He was with the foreign branch of the USDA—they've been sterilizing screwworm flies for the past thirty-five years or so."

"'Sterilizing screwworm flies,'" Jean repeated thoughtfully. "Uh-huh. I thought that's what you said. I don't think I'll even ask who did what to all those sterile screwworm flies, but I'm beginning to see why the two of them got together."

"Kilo Alpha works for the Department of Agriculture, too?"

"Kilo Alpha, as you call him, works for himself…if you call it working." Jean eyed the colorful straw purse Shea clutched under her shivering arm. "Wonder what's in the letter. Must be pretty important."

"It had better be," Shea said through chattering teeth.

They were still standing outside the heavy front door. Jean Cummings shifted her weight and said, "Look, this sounds too interesting to discuss out here on the porch with a Wilmington cabbie waiting. Why don't you pay him, and then I'll drop you in town later. Better yet, one of my boys has to drive to Wilmington today or tomorrow."

Grateful for any excuse to remain in one spot for a few minutes, Shea yielded with disgraceful eagerness. By the time she'd lugged her two massive suitcases to the porch Jean had unlocked the door. She brushed futilely at the wetness that had already started to soak through her coat and, visualizing warmth, comfort and even the possibility of a decent cup of coffee, gripped her two bags and wrestled them through the door.

The warmth that greeted her was strictly relative. It was an improvement over the blowing December rain, but just barely. At least she could relax for a few moments without worrying about falling asleep and missing her flight, or being crammed into a bus seat with another overfriendly man who smelled of garlic and cigars.

Where was Kilo Alpha, anyway? Looking around her at the gloomy elegance of dusty Honduras mahogany and worn Oriental rugs, she saw no sign of even a token Christmas decoration. No piñata, no wreath, not even a single candle, if one discounted the hurricane candles on the mantel. Evidently her elusive quarry was a bit of a Scrooge. She was beginning to understand why he and her grandfather had hit it off so well.

"Good thing for you I happened to be here," Jean Cummings declared. "Came over to bring in the mail and papers and to feed and walk Lady. Poor old gal needs her daily dose of TLC—misses Dave something awful. She won't eat at a kennel, and I respect her too much to expose her to my menagerie. I don't mind telling you, though, I'll be glad when that brother of mine gets back. It takes a whopping chunk out of my day to drive all the way out here and do the necessary, especially on a day like today. I had to practically push her out the door. Now tell me all about this letter."

He was out of town? She'd traveled five straight days and he was *out of town*? "The letter," Shea murmured, covering her dismay. "Granddad made me promise to deliver it by hand. It seemed so important to him there was no way I

could refuse." Her rueful smile said more than the few
sparse words. "So here I am."

"But why? I mean, why not just drop it in the mail? So it
might be delivered by water buffalo, it would get here eventually. And it's a helluva lot cheaper." Jean perched on the
faded chintz arm of a sofa and appraised her guest with
frank curiosity, taking in the signs of exhaustion that no
amount of suntan could hide, the shadowed eyes and the
thin, rumpled clothes. She glanced at the pair of bulging
suitcases. This woman obviously didn't believe in traveling
light.

"Dave's out of town on business," Jean said, sympathy
softening her normally brisk tones. "If you'd just let him
know you were coming—not that it would have done any
good. Any man who goes to business meetings in the middle of the Christmas holidays..." She shrugged.

An out-of-town business meeting. Shea knew an over-
powering feeling of frustration. For two cents she'd leave the
letter with Jean Cummings and forget she ever heard of Kilo
Alpha. She'd done her best to carry out her grandfather's
request, but this was getting to be absurd. "And you don't
know when he'll be back?" she asked, almost beyond caring.

"If he stays more than a couple of days I'll break his other
leg. He knows I've got my hands full with the party—we
always throw a big bash on New Year's Eve. Dammit, if I
didn't love that old mutt in there—" she nodded toward a
closed door "—I'd tell him to go jump." A low, keening
whimper lifted above the drumming sound of rain on the
metal roof. "Hear that? She knows we're talking about her.
Poor old thing's lonesome, and it tears me up to go off and
leave her, but what can I do? I'm three days behind on
everything."

Shea gnawed on her bottom lip. Surely it wouldn't be breaking her promise if she handed over the letter to Jean. And after all, the woman was his sister. That was the next best thing to delivering it to Kilo Alpha in person, wasn't it?

Jean slapped her forehead. "Oh, shoot, I forgot cat food! Honestly, it's a good thing my head's screwed on tight, or I'd walk off and forget that. Remind me to go back by the grocer's again when we leave here, will you?"

Shea's shoulders sagged. She couldn't do it. Not after coming this far. Besides, it wasn't as if she had to be anywhere else in particular. Once the letter was delivered she was free as a bird.

"You say your brother will be back in a few days?"

"Lord, he'd better be. He promised me faithfully he'd be here for the party. I've invited this woman I want him to meet. I got him a housekeeper once, and it was a disaster, so now I'm working on finding him a wife. I've got enough to keep up with without having to worry about Dave, too." Jean pushed a stack of rolled newspapers aside and flopped on the couch, lifting her feet to the coffee table. "Sit down, take a load off. You look as if you could stand to thaw out a minute while I try to remember what else it was I wanted from the hardware store. I keep making lists and forgetting to bring them with me. D'you ever do that? Comes from never having a minute's peace and quiet, I guess."

Hands deep in her pockets, Shea shivered while she waited for Jean to remember what she needed from the hardware store. What now? Hang around Southport until KA4ZDE showed up? Compared to boarding another bus or a plane, it didn't sound half bad. She was so tired that if she shut her eyes she'd probably sleep for a solid week.

"Where'd you get that tan?" Jean asked. Not waiting for an answer, she continued, "I used to tan like that twenty years and forty pounds ago."

Shea sneezed.

"Bless you." Jean swung her legs to the floor. "Cold in here, isn't it? We could go back in the kitchen where it's warm, but then Lady would get all excited again. She's so arthritic it hurts her just to wag her tail in this weather."

From her rapidly diminishing store of energy Shea managed a sympathetic smile. If this woman didn't do something—*anything*—soon she'd scream. She'd been traveling forever, and feeling more and more rotten each day. Something in the water, probably, although if she could once put down her bags and climb into a bed and just sleep the clock around she might just survive.

"The hardware store?" she prompted in an attempt to focus Jean's wandering mind long enough to get her off dead center.

"You need something there, too? I've got to stop by for an extension cord on my way home. Where you bound for, anyway?"

"At the moment I'm bound for the nearest hotel or rooming house where I can sleep until your brother gets back. After that . . . well, I haven't decided yet."

Jean's plump face sobered as she stared at the shivering form huddled in the oversized wing chair. "You're really wiped out, aren't you, honey? Is delivering that letter really so important to you?"

Shea nodded wordlessly. Hadn't she just finished saying so?

"Look, you're either coming down with something or you're asleep on your feet. Why don't you just leave the letter here on the mantel? Dave'll probably find it when he gets home. I'll try to remember to tell him about it, just to be sure."

"I'm fine, really. Just tired. I get airsick on planes and I can't seem to sleep on buses. All I need is a good night's sleep."

"Where exactly in Mexico did you come from?"

"A little village just outside Tuxtla Gutierrez. We lived in Tuxtla until Granddad retired. It's the capital of Chiapas." And when the older woman continued to stare at her as if she'd referred to one of the more obscure planets, she added, "Chiapas is down by the Guatemalan border. And by bus and plane, traveling without reservations during the holidays, it's five days' distance from Southport."

"Oh, my saints," Jean Cummings drawled reverently. "And you came all this way just to deliver a letter? Honey, this beats anything I ever heard. No wonder you're— Five days, you said? No wonder you're bushed! You're not going back there to—to wherever it was, are you?"

Shea shook her head. "I've moved back to the States for good."

"Whereabouts? Have you still got family here in the States?" Jean shook her head. "Nothing like having a stranger bombard you with personal questions, is there? I'm so used to grilling my kids that I forget to turn it off when I'm out in polite society."

"No problem." Shea managed a weak grin. Actually, it was rather nice having someone show concern for her welfare. "At the moment, I don't mind telling you I could take root right here in this chair with a little encouragement."

Jean lowered her feet with a thump, scattering clumps of wet sand from her rubberized moccasins. "Let's get you fixed up before you topple over, then. Forget Dave's letter until you're feeling better. I wouldn't subject you to a meeting with him for anything. He's bad enough at the best of times, but since he's been in a cast he's impossible."

In a cast and off on a business trip. Having just run the gamut of holiday travelers, she could sympathize with him. There were times when she'd have traded her suitcases for a cast. At least he could cadge a ride in a wheelchair. She'd started out with a set of wheels for her heaviest case, but one of them had broken off, making the remaining one worse than useless.

"If you could just drop me off at a hotel? There is one, isn't there?" she asked diffidently.

"Motels—two or three, but I'm not leaving you at any motel alone in this condition. You're coming home with me."

"That's kind of you, Jean, but I wouldn't dream of imposing. All I need is a place to park my luggage and catch up on my sleep, and I'll be fine."

Jean grabbed one of the bags and headed for the front door, and Shea had little choice but to follow. She flinched from the blast of damp, cold wind that flattened her thin clothes against her body. She was either going to have to hibernate or get herself something warm to wear, and at the moment, hibernation sounded far more appealing.

Once inside the steamy warmth of the pickup truck, she fought a losing battle with sleep. Now that she was no longer plagued by motion sickness, she couldn't seem to hold her eyes open. Jean hummed tunelessly under her breath, and Shea muttered something about dropping her off in town.

The next thing she knew, they were pulling up before a rambling cedar-shake ranch building surrounded by an assortment of vehicles. Two lanky, towheaded boys were shooting baskets in the rain.

"Welcome to Oak Island. We've got a houseful with Biff home for the holidays and the neighbor's kids in and out all the time, but there's always room for one more. I'm going to tuck you in and let you sleep until starvation gets you up again.''

Shea managed a halfhearted protest, only to be shushed. ''Honey, if I dropped you off at a motel I'd just be worrying about you, running into town to check up on you, and believe me, it's all I can do to keep up with my own brood and make it out to Dave's once a day. The boys won't go near the place in case he gets back and asks one of 'em to drive him around. They took turns when he was plastered up to the hip.''

''Jean, you don't even *know* me.'' Shea protested, but she was too tired to make an issue of it. What could it hurt? She couldn't help but trust Jean, stranger or not, and she could use a friend.

Psychologically, as well as practically, this was a bad time to be rootless and on the road. For years she'd made plans for the time when she'd be free to live her life the way she wanted to, without a loving, if chauvinistic and overprotective grandfather directing every move she made. Now that the time had actually come, she found that she was tired, lonely, scared, and she missed her grandfather badly.

''Honey, what you need is a nice hot soak, a good meal and a warm bed. If I can take care of a husband, five sons, four dogs, four cats, two ferrets and my brother's old mutt, the least I can do is feed you and give you a bed to collapse in before someone has to sweep you up off the street.''

Twenty-four hours later Shea was nursing a mug of steaming cocoa and watching Jean crack the whip over the Cummings circus. She'd been introduced to an enormous cast of characters, some of whom were Cummingses, some of whom were visitors. Of the assortment of pets, the only ones whose names she could recall were Cranberry, the Irish setter, and Sherlock and Watson, the ferrets.

"Keep your shoes on," Jean warned. "The boys tease them with their feet, and they nip at anything that even looks like a toe."

Shea curled her toes inside her loosely woven huaraches. "Jean, is there a place where I could get a few things to wear? I wasn't even thinking about clothes when I set off on this wild-goose chase."

"I'll drop you off while I pick up a few more things for the party, and then we'll ride out to Dave's and see if he's shown up yet. Honestly, I don't know how long I can keep up this routine. Before I get breakfast dishes in to soak it's time to start dinner. As for lunch, it's a continuous process, and now there's the party. Did you ever have a day when nothing went right? It's been one of those winters."

Sipping her cocoa, Shea nodded. It had been one of those winters for her, as well, but at least she was nearing the end of it.

"Everybody looks forward to a little something extra at our annual New Year's Eve party, but wouldn't you know it? The fortune-teller I booked last July picked this week to come down with appendicitis, and the best I can do at this late date is a dog act." Planting wet, sudsy hands on her hips, Jean hooted. "Can you see my bringing a dog act into this house? Talk about storm damage! Chan, put your brother's car keys back and take the truck," she admonished her middle son.

"But Ma, I'm going to pick up my woman!" the gangly, white-haired youth protested. Over supper last night Shea had heard all about the car his parents had refused to give sixteen-year-old Chan for Christmas—something called a "Z," the lack of which would blight his social standing forever.

"Joey's fourteen and Lee's just a year behind," Jean explained. "I don't know which is going to be worse, trying to keep 'em all in college or trying to keep 'em all on wheels. What little they earn when they're not in school doesn't go that far, but, then, what does these days?''

Shea wondered as much, not for the first time since she'd left Mexico. While the three youngest Cummings boys argued the merits of the dog act over a local rock group she considered her own situation. Would her funds last long enough to see her established somewhere with enough supplies to get her started again? With the peso so devalued they'd been able to live fairly well in Chiapas on a dollar income, but here in the States it might be a different matter. Travel had already made alarming inroads into her carefully budgeted savings.

She sipped her cocoa, missing the cinnamon she was accustomed to. After twelve hours of sleep on a horizontal, nonmoving surface she felt a hundred percent better. Jean had even managed to keep the parade of animals at bay until almost eight o'clock that morning. The cry, "Ferret on the loose," was not exactly conducive to further rest.

Already her tan was beginning to fade, Shea noted, flexing her fingers experimentally. Absently she touched a tiny scar on her palm that ended in a callus at the base of her forefinger. Silverworking was rough on the hands; the slip of a file had lengthened her heart line by half an inch or more. Inez would have concocted some wild, improbable story to account for even that.

Until she'd gone to live with her daughter, Inez had been Ed Bellwood's housekeeper. Her gift of laughter and her zeal for the mysteries of life had opened new worlds for a hurt and frightened child. With Shea's best interests at heart, her grandfather had done his best to root out any weaknesses she might have inherited from her artist mother. He'd seen that she had a solid, conservative education with secretarial training to ensure her future.

Inez, on the other hand, had taken her to the various markets and introduced her to the craftsmen who produced the lovely filigreed silverwork for which the area was famous. She'd filled her head with lovely folktales and superstititions and taught her the basics of palmistry. She'd been hinting at an education in astrology when her daughter had given birth to twins and called for help.

"You have the hands of an old soul," Inez had been fond of saying. At the moment Shea felt far more like an old body, never mind soul.

"Come on, Ma, it's no big deal," Lee was saying. "Nobody believes that old fortune-telling junk, anyway."

"Don't feed that dog at the table. It's traditional. We've had a fortune-teller every year for the past—"

"Hey, we could get a woman to dress up in a diaper and be the Baby New Year. Earl Peacock had one at his party last year and she was terrific!"

"Earl Peacock wears a gold earring, too," Jean said crushingly. "Maybe we could have an ear-piercing party." She placed her foot against the setter's rump and shoved in the direction of the door. "Scram, you big moocher. You boys feed that dog another bite in this kitchen and *I'll* tell your fortunes for you. Believe me, they'll curl your hair!"

Shea tuned out the good-natured wrangling and concentrated on her next move. She had to make a decision. Any day now she'd be free of her obligation, and when that time came, she needed to be ready to move on.

"Would you, Shea?"

She looked up at the expectant ring of faces surrounding her. "Would I what?"

"Would you mind doubling up with Karen?" Biff explained. "I'm picking her up at the airport at four, and if you two can share, then when Bucky gets here, he can—"

"Whoa, wait a minute," Shea exclaimed. "I'm not staying."

Jean's voice rose over Shea's. "Bucky! Who's Bucky?"

Shea hurried on. "I mean, you've all been just great, but I wouldn't think of intruding. I was too tired to argue with your mother yesterday, but I'm planning to get a room at a motel this morning."

The ragged chorus of dismay cut through her like a hot knife through butter. There was no mistaking the boys' sincerity, in spite of the fact that she'd used more than her share of hot water last night showering and shampooing the travel grime away, in spite of the fact that her unexpected arrival had caused a shift in the dormitorylike sleeping arrangements. "I can't stay here," she pleaded gently. "You don't even know me."

"Not in the biblical sense." That from Biff, the college freshman.

Jean cut him off with a snort. "First year out of the nest and he thinks he's God's gift to women. I'm warning you, boy, you sleep in the east room and Karen sleeps in the west, and if I hear the patter of little feet going down that hallway—"

"It'll be Sherlock and Watson," Lee the youngest, put in. The ferrets were his, and while they were supposed to be kept on a leash, they seldom were. Their progress through the house was usually marked by a trail of uprooted houseplants and scattered sofa pillows.

Jean lifted her hand in mock threat, and Shea laughed. Then, staring at the broad, capable palm, she sobered. She'd been wondering how she could repay the Cummingses for their hospitality. Perhaps there was a way, after all. Could she? She'd never done it before, but she'd picked up a lot just from listening to Inez over the years. She'd even read a few books on the subject as a matter of idle interest.

And she certainly owed her hostess a debt of gratitude. Left to her own devices, she'd probably have slept a week, not bothering to eat, and waked up with pneumonia.

"Would a palmist do?" she asked diffidently.

"Would a palmist do what?" Joey, the fourteen-year-old, asked.

Shea waited until the rest of the chorus diminished, and then she made her hesitant offer.

"You're kidding! You're a real palmist? Read mine!" Chan demanded, sticking a grease-stained hand under her nose. "See how long I'm going to have to put up with that old rusted-out piece of junk before I can get a decent set of wheels."

"Boys, boys, sit down and shut up a minute, will you? Chandler, I want you to go by your Uncle Dave's today and walk Lady for me, all right?"

"But, Ma, my woman's expecting me."

"Your woman can wait. Besides, unless you've changed women since last week, she's helping her mama make candy today." Jean turned to Shea, a speculative gleam in her eyes. "Shea, if you know the difference between a palm and a knuckle and can fake the rest, you're on. Nobody really cares as long as you wear a turban and look mysterious. I'd planned to drape a few curtains in a corner and make a little tent, just for atmosphere. We'll throw in candlelight, incense, the works."

Shea drew in her shoulders, already regretting her hasty offer. Maybe she could just wash dishes for a few days, instead. "Maybe you could play charades."

"Charades," three of the boys protested in disgust.

"I don't really know that much about it. I mean, I've read a few books and I had a friend once who was a firm believer, but—" Shea's feet were getting colder by the moment.

"You'll be terrific," Jean declared, neatly cutting off her hesitant efforts to wiggle out of the impulsive offer. "We'll bill you as Madame . . . Hmm." She jutted her chin and assumed a faraway look. "Shea doesn't sound mysterious enough. How about Madame Moonlight?"

There was a chorus of sounds that, interpreted loosely, meant yuk.

"Starlight?" Jean offered.

"How about LaZonga?"

"How about Lasagna?"

"How about Spaghetti?"

"Boys!" Jean screeched. She turned to Shea, who had tactfully remained silent, and announced breezily, "Never mind, we've got three days to come up with your professional name. Meanwhile, I did some thinking last night, and I've got the solution to all our problems. Yours and mine and Lady's."

Two

There were a dozen reasons to say no and only two possible reasons why she should even consider it. Nevertheless, later that day, Shea found herself getting settled into David Pendleton's house, making the acquaintance of an arthritic Shetland sheepdog and an antique heating system.

Pendle Hall had obviously been a showplace in its time. Surrounded by massive oaks, magnolias and cedars, the house managed to look both regal and shabby, like a down-on-her-luck dowager. Tall and perfectly square, it had once been white, but badly needed painting. A wide porch that wrapped as far as she could see did little to soften the bleak facade—nor did the four tall, brick chimneys that, along with the steep tin roof, gleamed darkly in the drizzling rain. Out beyond the house, past several sagging outbuildings and an upturned boat, the pewter surface of the Cape Fear River gleamed dully through the trees.

"I'll just sort of camp out, okay?" she said diffidently to Jean, who ignored her to peer into several kitchen cabinets.

"Look at this jumble, would you? Just because the last housekeeper I found for him didn't pan out, he refuses to trust me to find him another one." Jean shrugged, yanked open a drawer, held up a heavily tarnished fork and shook her head. "Mama'd have a fit if she could see the state her silver was in."

Shea glanced at the fork. The ornate design was all but obscured by tarnish. As someone who had come to respect silver in any form, she hated to see such signs of neglect. She'd kept the baroque Bellwood silver well polished even before her grandfather had given it to her. "Why not take the silver home with you?" She knew that Pendle Hall had once been Jean's home, as well. "Not that it's any business of mine, but if your brother doesn't want to be bothered, he could hardly complain."

"Don't look at me," Jean said quickly. "I'm not into silver polishing, or heirlooms, either. Give me unbreakable dishes and good serviceable stainless steel any day." She slammed the drawer shut. "Did I show you where Lady's mash is kept? You mix it with warm water and whatever leftovers you have on hand."

"Look, Jean, are you sure we're doing the right thing?" They'd already gone through all the arguments pro and con, but now that Shea was actually here, moving into a stranger's house without his knowledge, it seemed . . . well, if not actually unethical, certainly uncomfortable.

"One small step for Dave's dog, one giant step for my sanity," Jean paraphrased. "As long as Lady likes you, you haven't got a worry in the world. Dave doesn't give a hoot about this old mausoleum. His dog, his work, that's all he cares about. Sometimes I wonder if he really cares about his work all that much." She opened another door and closed it quickly, shaking her head. "Pete calls him a loner. I'd hate to tell you what I've called him on occasion, especially since he broke his leg."

"You're not making me feel a bit better about this," Shea said with a small laugh. "Maybe I'd better—"

"Oh, don't listen to me," Jean said hurriedly, as if seeing her last chance for deliverance slip away. "You know how it is with brothers and sisters. Look, Shea, I've got to run now, but I'll check with you this afternoon just to be sure you've settled in all right. Jeep's in the back, key's in a pigeonhole in the secretary, if you need to go anywhere. And honey, don't look so forlorn. Dave'll be so glad to know Lady's had someone to look after her he might even manage to be civil."

"Oh, my, you *are* reassuring."

Jean laughed. "Just kidding. Actually, he's a pretty terrific guy under that crust of his."

"But that crust goes all the way through, right?"

Misgivings began to close in on Shea as she watched the muddy blue pickup bounce off down the driveway. It had all sounded so reasonable when Jean had explained the situation. As the mother of five sons and Lord knows how many strays, up to her neck in social and civic affairs, not to mention a big party in three days' time, the daily trips to care for a slow-moving old dog took more time than she could easily spare. As long as Shea was determined to go the last mile and deliver that letter in person then she needed a place to stay, and David Pendleton had all these rooms just going to waste.

At least Lady seemed thrilled to have someone in constant attendance, if the flap of her tail and the look in her clouded eyes were anything to go by. Canine toenails clicked slowly across the hardwood floor, and Shea opened her hand to receive the cold nose. "This is the hand that's going to be

feeding you, girl, so don't bite it. And remember, when and
if your master shows up, you're going to put in a good word
for me, aren't you?''

One at a time, Shea carried her suitcases up the wide,
gracefully balustraded stairway. Of the four bedrooms Jean
had shown her, she'd chosen the smallest. She'd unpack
only enough to get by with. That way she'd be ready to slam
both cases shut and be on her way the minute she'd turned
the letter over to the addressee.

Out of respect for the privacy of her unwitting host, Shea
made a fetish of keeping to as few rooms as possible. She
took her meals in the kitchen, despite the rather doggy
smell, and at night she sat in the living room, reading one of
the few novels she'd discovered among the hundreds of
nonfiction titles. The book wasn't all that interesting, but at
least it was something to keep her mind off the strange
noises in the isolated old house.

She also read the two newspapers that were delivered
daily, as well as the ones that had accumulated, carefully
refolding them afterward and leaving them in the proper
order on the secretary beside the growing stack of mail.

Oddly enough, she was beginning to feel almost at home,
if not in the gloomy old mansion, at least in the region itself. Walking Lady through acres of overgrown riverside
gardens, shopping in the friendly little town of Southport—even reading the local papers. Without quite knowing how it had come about, she'd begun to get a definite feel
for the area.

Jean's phone calls helped, too. Breezy, friendly, she was
never too busy to stop and chat for a few minutes.

"What do I do when Lady wants to come upstairs?" Shea
had asked that first night. "Is she allowed?"

"She's allowed anywhere her feeble old bones can take her, but you'll have to carry her down if she gets up. She's never been able to go downstairs."

Surrounded by her absent host's belongings—the elegant, if slightly shabby furniture, the overflowing bookshelves, the pair of matching leather wing chairs, only one of which was really worn—Shea found herself thinking of David Pendleton rather a lot.

She chose to sit in the other wing chair, the one that looked as if it had hardly been used, but often she'd glance up from her book at its mate, seeing the sunken cushions, the shiny place across the shoulders, the indentations on one wing. She could almost picture a graying head nodding there while a book slid to the floor unheeded.

Poor lonely old man. Shea had stayed on in Mexico all these years because of another such lonely old man. Jean hadn't mentioned her brother's age, but from his description, he was probably older than her admitted forty-seven years—possibly much older. After all, he'd been her grandfather's friend for as long as Shea could remember.

On the day of the party, Shea scanned the newspaper, paying particular attention to help-wanted ads, fine-craft outlets and real estate. The future that had seemed so nebulous only a little while ago was already here. And the choice, for the first time in her twenty-three years, was hers. Should she do as her grandfather had planned and look for a job as a secretary?

"Teaching, nursing, or office work—those are your best bets, child. A woman can always find work if she's properly trained."

By the time she was old enough to take her choice of *his* choices, Shea had known exactly what she wanted to do. She'd also known that it would only aggravate her grandfather's heart condition if she insisted on following in her mother's flamboyant footsteps. Mia had been a painter, a sculptor, a set-designer and a fashion designer, with varying degrees of success. When last heard from, she'd been living in Paris designing hats that sold for a small fortune.

According to Edward Bellwood, who'd lost his wife years before Shea had come to live with him, it had been Mia and her wild, reckless ways that had been responsible for the ruin of his only son, Willis.

Shea had been twelve when she'd been sent to live in Mexico. She'd been unable to defend either of her parents after years of watching in silent agony as they all but destroyed each other.

Mia and Willis had started living together as college students in the late sixties, both espousing every wild cause that had come along. Only after Shea was born had they married. As Mia was fond of telling her friends, she'd try anything once—even marriage.

Neither marriage nor motherhood had changed her hedonistic life-style. Willis, on the other hand, had eventually shed his beard, donned a three-piece suit and landed himself a job near Savannah, Georgia. Shea hadn't known for a long time just how much he'd hated it.

Before she was even old enough to understand the hateful words that echoed through the thin-walled rooms, she'd found her own way of dealing with a reality she was powerless to change. When the fights began, she'd simply close her bedroom door, put on a tape of her favorite music and doodle for hours, covering page after page with intricate, meaningless designs.

The fights had increased in frequency and volume, the invective growing crueler with each one. And then one day Willis quit his job, packed a bag and walked out. Mia, left with a daughter she'd never taken the time to get to know, had been stunned and then furious with herself for not having the good sense to leave first.

That had been the beginning of a new life for Shea. The grandfather she'd never met had accepted her without question, moving into a larger house so that his housekeeper could live with them. Within a matter of months, Shea had been able to eat a whole meal without that awful gnawing pain in her stomach. By the time she'd lived in Tuxtla for a year she'd even learned not to flinch at loud voices.

Her tall, scholarly grandfather had given her a steady, healing sort of love, with emphasis on practical guidance. Inez, small and round and noisily demonstrative, had given her love of another sort, laughing or scolding, depending on the needs of the moment.

Shea would miss them both, but they'd taught her well. She'd breezed through her business courses, but she'd also studied art. Later, over her grandfather's expressed disapproval, she'd apprenticed with an excellent silversmith, learning to work both the precious metal and various semiprecious stones.

It had been the one time she'd gone against his wishes. He'd rationalized it by comparing it with his avid interest in amateur radio. "Oh, well, just as a hobby, I don't suppose it will do any lasting harm," he'd conceded.

Whatever the future held for her, Shea considered herself well prepared. If she was lucky, she'd be a silversmith with enough business ability to manage her own affairs. If not, she'd be a secretary with a fascinating, if rather expensive hobby. The only thing that remained to be seen was where this future of hers would take place.

Once the rain stopped and the clouds cleared away, Shea found it impossible to remain inside. Against the clear turquoise sky, gulls circled out over the river. Gray-green beards of Spanish moss swayed gently under the live-oak trees. Wearing jeans, boots and the padded jacket she'd purchased in town, Shea took the old dog for a walk, following a trail that led down to the marshy edge of the Cape Fear River. Together they sat on the trunk of a pine that had been uprooted in a recent hurricane and watched a freighter being guided upriver to Wilmington by one of the Southport pilots. She was growing fonder of the area with each passing day.

Jean called just as Shea sat down to lunch. "Still no word from Dave. If that man doesn't show up for my party I'm going to tan his hide! I've been singing his praises to Connie—I told you I'd invited her to meet him, didn't I?"

"You mentioned it. I expect he'll show up in time if he knows he has a date."

"Who, Dave?" Jean hooted. "You've got to be kidding. That man's about as reliable as a three-dollar raincoat."

"Surely he has a job to come back to, or is he retired?"

"If you call writing books a job," Jean scoffed. "The nonfiction kind. Not that I've read any of them. Brother or no brother, if there's no sex in it, I'm not going to waste my good reading time wading through any book."

An author. That would explain the extensive reference library.

Jean rambled on, and Shea took a bite of her sandwich and pinched off a bite for Lady while she waited for Jean to arrive at the point of the phone call. There was always a point to Jean's calls. In just the few days she'd known her, Shea had learned that much.

"At a moment's notice," the older woman was saying. "Dad died while Dave was in his junior year at Duke, and since I was pregnant, as usual, poor old Dave got saddled with all the estate business. It was a mess, believe me. They'd never got along too well, either, and that didn't help much. Afterward Dave dropped out of school and took off on a motorcycle, said he was going to find the Pan-American Highway and ride the thing all the way to the bottom of the continent."

"Did he?"

"Beats me. He was gone long enough, but my brother's not the chatty type. Funny that he should end up being a ham operator, isn't it?"

Shea shrugged and handed the rest of her lunch to the dog. "Oh, I don't know. Maybe he's like Granddad and prefers long-distance relationships."

"Might be a point," Jean replied. "Look, I called about your costume. Have you got anything really far out? I mean turban, shawl, maybe a little cleavage and a lot of junk jewelry?"

"The jewelry's no problem, at least. I've been working in silver for several years now, and besides that, I have a few of my grandmother's things. As for the rest, I think I can improvise. I've got several embroidered, handwoven things."

"Terrific! Biff knocked together a frame for my old dining-room draperies, so your office awaits you, Madame Houdini."

Shea laughed. "Sorry, I think that one's been taken. Try again."

"Hey, we'll call you Madame Sapphire. Those navy eyes of yours could pass for gypsy eyes with a little makeup."

"I'll do my best, but as for makeup, I never bothered much beyond lipstick. Maybe I could wear a mask."

"Don't you dare! I'd sell my second son for your looks, but maybe you'd better dig into my paints. You look a little too sweet and innocent to be dealing in deep, dark secrets."

Laughing, Shea visualized her pleasant, if unexciting features, the thick, glossy dark-brown hair she wore in a

simple short cut. "Oh, thanks a lot. For sweet and innocent, read dull and gullible."

"Gullible, maybe. Any woman who'd let herself be talked
into doing what you did might be a little soft around the
edges, but never dull, honey. Dull is *not* having the gump-
tion to tackle such a fool project. By the way," she dropped
in casually, "do you think you could come over early? I've
got a million last minute things to do, and I'd hoped I could
steal time to give myself a facial and do my nails. Once a
year I go all out—bubble bath, eye shadow, the whole bit."

By the time she was dressed and ready to go, Shea had
developed a serious case of butterflies. She'd half expected
David Pendleton to walk in on her any moment, and as a
consequence, she'd been unable to relax. Lady, her movements less stiff now that the weather had grown warmer and
dryer, watched as she reached for the bag of mash.

"What on earth have I gotten myself into, Lady?" She
measured out the kibbles, adding some leftover soup and a
little warm milk. At fourteen, Lady hadn't much left to
chew with. "I've never seriously read a palm in my life."

It was only a party trick, of course. Still, she was beginning to regret her impulsive offer. She owed the Cummingses for their hospitality, but surely house-sitting and
looking after Lady took care of that.

When Mike came for her, she was dressed in a colorful
handloomed-and-embroidered skirt she'd bought in Tehu-
atepac, a navy turtleneck top and several of her favorite
pieces of jewelry. Her cleavage, she'd decided, wouldn't
have been all that exciting. She'd packed another length of
handloomed fabric for a turban and an embroidered *huipil*
to pull on over her skirt. Along with a strand of her grandmother's crystal-and-jet beads that her grandfather had
given her on her sixteenth birthday, she selected one or two

of her showier pieces and an enormous pair of dangle earrings.

"Hey, you look great, Shea. You better cram down all the food you can before things get started," Mike warned, "'cause once they do, you won't have time to eat. I've told everybody about you, and I know at least a hundred people who want their palms read tonight."

"A hundred! How big is this party, anyway?" Shea asked as she signaled for Lady to stay.

"Just the usual gang—that's half of Southport and all of Oak Island, from Caswell all the way to Folly's End. And Dad's invited a few people down from Wilmington."

Shea had thought at the time he must be joking. Several hours later, as she looked up from the small round table tucked beneath an open tent that bore the crayoned legend Madame Blueskies to see the long line of customers waiting for her services, she wasn't so certain. Surely these people weren't seriously expecting her to read their fortunes in the palms of their hands!

Subduing the small access of panic, Shea concentrated on the hand of a man who'd earlier been introduced to her as a stockbroker. In the rare event that she ever accumulated enough to invest in the market, she'd definitely avoid this man's services. He was supposed to *know* where the fortunes were. Her forefinger trailed down his palm, following a vertical line that splintered off just past midway. Judging his age to be somewhere in the midthirties, she intoned solemnly, "I see a change of career in store for you, one that's not entirely unrelated to your present career."

The hand clenched as though to cover its secrets, then unfolded again. "Keep your voice down, lady. These are some of my best clients. You want to start a stampede?"

Rattled, Shea switched abruptly to the heart line, noticed the pronounced chaining effect and grabbed his thumb, instead. "Your temper—you have a tendency to bottle things up inside you too much." She touched the thick padding at the base of the appendage. "Energy stored here in the mound of Venus flows through here." Indicating a short, wasted middle joint, she moved on to the bulbous nail joint. "But it's dammed up here. It can burst out explosively unless you learn to control it. Think twice before speaking," she warned gravely, lowering eyelids heavy with layers of shadow and mascara. "Think even longer before taking action." Dropping the hand, she stepped back to indicate that the reading was ended.

She lowered her head and took a deep breath. She'd all but recovered from the exhaustion of traveling. This was exhaustion of another kind. Amazing how much emotional energy could be transferred through the touch of a hand, and not all of it soothing. She'd concentrated so hard on remembering the things she'd learned from Inez or read about in the dog-eared old books on palmistry she'd borrowed years ago that she'd forgotten the human element.

She hadn't counted on the way intuition took over, so that she heard herself saying things she wasn't even aware of having learned. Not always, not with every hand, but often enough so that she was thoroughly shaken. After the first few times it had happened she'd tried deliberately holding herself aloof, but then, with no warning at all, it would come at her again, that disturbing flow of energy, as though she were connected on some atavistic level with the person whose hand she held.

Shea caught sight of her reflection in the mirror. It was like seeing a stranger...the colorful, exotic costume, the heavy makeup. She did rather look the part, didn't she?

Madame Blueskies. They'd finally compromised on that one. Somewhere in the back of Shea's mind, the name was all mixed up with clouds and rain and sudden clearings, an omen of sorts. Inez would have understood.

"But it doesn't even sound like a palmist, Shea," Jean had complained.

"That makes it all the more mysterious, then, doesn't it?" Shea had reasoned, tired of all the fanciful sobriquets suggested by the Cummings clan.

She assumed what she hoped was a look of ageless wisdom and reached for the next palm. Sooner or later she'd be finished here, and then she'd slip away, get herself something to eat and see if one of the boys could drive her home. Tomorrow was the first day of a new year, and she'd wasted enough time already. Letter or no letter, she'd contact a realtor and see if there was a chance of finding affordable housing in the area.

"What do you mean, you've got someone living in my house?" David tossed his crutch aside and leaned against the bar, his eyes boring into the top of Jean's lacquered head. "Look at me, dammit, are you telling me that you turned over the keys to my house to a perfect stranger and you *haven't been out there since*? God, by now I probably don't even have a house!"

When Jean continued to stuff smoked turkey into hot croissants as if he weren't even there, he lurched across to lean on the counter, chin jutting dangerously as he warned, "Stop stonewalling me, Jean, I'm serious. According to Pete, you picked some girl up off the streets and brought her home with you. With a houseful of boys, yet! Good God, where's your common sense?"

"I did not pick her up off the streets," Jean retorted calmly. "She came out to your house while I was there feeding Lady, and—"

"And that didn't tip you off? A stranger snooping around an empty house? Why didn't you invite her inside?" His sarcasm went unanswered. In dawning horror he said slowly, "You did invite her inside. Knowing you, you probably even gave her a guided tour."

"Yep. She was horrified by the silverware, by the way. Hasn't been polished in years, from the looks of it."

Dave's shoulders sagged tiredly. "The silverware. You mean what's left of it after that thieving old witch of a housekeeper you sicced on me got through with it. She was hauling away stuff by the truckload!"

"Oh, it wasn't that bad," Jean dismissed. "You always did try to make things sound worse than they are."

"Things can't get much worse than they are," Dave grumbled, arguing more from force of habit than any real hope of winning. It had been a rotten week and his leg hurt, and to come home and find some little floozy installed in his house… "Why didn't you just hand over the key to my safe while you were at it?"

"She didn't ask for it." Jean didn't bat an eye. She'd been dealing with the male animal too many years to be bothered by her brother's irascibility. Pete had picked him up at the airport and brought him directly here on Jean's orders. "Dave, go comb your hair, will you? I've got someone I want you to meet. She's a widow, about your age, good-looking and owns her own business. You could do worse."

Dave offered a pithy remark and downed the whiskey someone had left on the counter. "No," he said flatly.

"Just meet her, that's all I ask. I more or less promised her you'd be her date tonight, but—"

"Jean, is there a legal term for a brother murdering a sister?"

"Sistercide? Which reminds me, I haven't explained about Shea."

"You know what you can do with your women?" Dave said nastily. Reaching up, he began to knead the tight muscles at the back of his neck. What man could ever hope to win out over a sister who was fifteen years his senior. She'd changed his diapers too many times, and she never hesitated to remind him of that fact. "By the way, I'll need one of the boys to drive me around until I get rid of this cast. Biff's home from school, isn't he?"

"Forget it. He's got a new girlfriend visiting him."

Dave grunted. "Mike, then."

"He's bagging at the Red and White. Sorry. By the way, did you have a nice time in New York?"

He shot her a dirty look. "You've never broken anything, have you, Jean?"

"Not so much as a promise," Jean replied pleasantly, licking her fingers and lifting the tray of turkey rolls. "Have a roll and another drink, honey. In fact, have a couple of drinks. May as well celebrate, seeing as someone will have to haul you home, anyway."

"About this woman," Dave began.

"Which one, Shea or Connie?"

Someone wearing a party hat leaned in through the doorway. "Hey, Jean, got any more black olives?"

"In a minute," Jean promised. She turned back to the man who stood glowering at her. "About Shea—"

"Where do you keep your mops, Jean?" someone else inquired. "At least it was the white wine, not the red."

Closing her eyes momentarily, Jean indicated the pantry. She took a deep breath. "Look, we can't talk here. Let me go out there and see if they've completely dismantled the place. I'll try to round up Connie. Meanwhile, if you get a chance, introduce yourself to Madame Blueskies."

"Hey, Jean!" This from the living room.

"Coming! Go get your fortune told," she ordered hurriedly.

"I don't want my fortune told. I just want to go home!"

"Oh, go on," Jean urged. "You'll like her. She's really great." She made her escape quickly before she could receive the blessings her brother called down upon her innocent head.

Shea closed her eyes momentarily and braced herself to face the next extended palm. Surely she was reaching the end of the line. She'd been at it for hours.

"I suppose you have a license for this sort of thing, Madame Blueskies?"

It all hit her at once, the familiar drawl, the scent of smoky cologne, the sight of an enormous sock-clad cast protruding from the slit leg of a pair of threadbare cords.

"KA4ZDE?" It was the voice that triggered the response. How many times had she heard that voice coming into her kitchen via the bank of radios mounted on one wall?

This was David Pendleton? This angry, injured giant? But this was no contemporary of her grandfather's. Even with the scowl he looked years younger than Jean.

Dave's eyes narrowed at the unexpected greeting. Either she was a damned sight smoother than most of these fakes, or someone had been priming her. As long as he was stuck here at this brawl until someone could drive him home, he might as well see how much they'd told her. Wouldn't be the first time he'd been set up, and at least it was better than being shoved at whatever female Jean was trying to foist off on him this time.

Laying his crutch aside, he prepared to lower himself on to the chair opposite the dark, garishly painted little hustler.

"Hey, man, get to the back of the line," someone called out.

"Yeah, Dave, just because you're all busted up, that doesn't give you any special privileges. Madame Blueskies has been waiting to hold my hand all night, haven't you, honey?"

Grunting a curse under his breath, Dave reached for his stick. When his turn came, he didn't want half of Southport breathing down his neck. He'd obviously been set up but good. He'd get Jean for this. Dammit, enough was enough! And here she came now, bearing down on him with a predatory-looking redhead.

"I'll see you later," he promised, impaling Shea with a look that left her thoroughly rattled as he made his escape through a side door.

Good Lord, this was the man she'd come all the way across the country to see?

Shea followed his progress across the crowded room. People automatically cleared the way for a man with a crutch. She suspected they'd have cleared a path for David Pendleton, crutch or no crutch. Even from the back he looked imposing—something about the arrogant set of his head, no doubt. Or the shoulders. Were they really that broad, or was it just the contrast with those narrow, muscular hips that made them seem eight feet wide?

Why had she assumed he was an old man? If there was any gray in his sun-streaked brown hair, it wasn't evident in the dim light. But, then, she'd been practically mesmerized by the spell of his topaz eyes. Not the color, although that was striking enough in the rugged matrix of his long, craggy face, but the fiery accusation she'd seen there, as though he'd caught her with her hand in his pocket.

At the thought of her hand actually sliding into the pocket of those close-fitting pants she shuddered. Then, breathing deeply, she closed her eyes for a moment to regather her composure before opening them to the palm of her next client.

It was an easy one this time, thank goodness. An average man who'd led an average life and would probably go on doing so for years to come. Tactfully avoiding the word "average," Shea played up the small things as palm after palm was extended for her examination. After a while, she almost succeeded in forgetting the man who stood glowering, drink in hand, just outside her line of vision.

It was almost midnight by the time she finished. Sagging in exhaustion, Shea let her mind go blank for a long moment. Anything she still owed the Cummingses for taking her in and befriending her had been paid in full. Next time the occasion arose, she wouldn't be so quick to offer her services as a reader of palms. That impulsive streak of hers would definitely need to be toned down if she didn't want to land herself in hot water.

Goodness, had Inez gone through this—this emotional buffeting everytime she'd reached for Shea's hand and traced the lines with a yellowed-and-wrinkled forefinger? Shea had taken it lightly, thinking it was all a game. She was no longer quite so certain.

"And now perhaps you'd care to read my palm, Madame Gypsy."

The drawl was only slightly more pronounced than it had been an hour ago, but the warm scent of Scotch mingled with a subtle after-shave touched Shea's nostrils, making her wary. Her eyes touched on the palm David Pendleton placed on the table and skittered away again, as if by avoiding the sight of him she could avoid facing the complicated issue between them. She was too tired for long-winded explanations. Besides, she had an idea that Kilo Alpha was not going to be the most reasonable man in the world.

"What's the matter, Madame Blueskies, have you forgotten your lines? I should think a good memory would be crucial in a scam like this."

Stifling a groan, Shea lowered her eyes to his hand. It was a strong hand, the vigor of its square palm and long, widespread fingers marking it as one of the so-called intellectual types. Suddenly she was shaken by a powerful reaction that seemed rooted in the deepest levels of her consciousness. Her senses unusually attuned to the vital force that seemed to surround the man, she could actually feel the heat of his eyes as they touched on her gaudy turban and lingered on the enormous dangling earrings.

"Well? Come on, gypsy woman, read my fortune." It was both a dare and a taunt, and Shea slipped her hand under the outstretched palm.

"Yours is a—" She cleared her throat as her fingers tightened involuntarily around the back of his hand. "Yours is what we call an intellectual hand," she said with a calmness that belied the tremors that raced through her whole body. "The square palm, the long fingers, the—ah..." She swallowed audibly. She could feel the crisp strands of hair against his finely textured skin. Her own palm grew moist. "It's—it's quite flexible, you see. It's sometimes referred to as the air type. As opposed to fire, earth and water, that is."

She made the mistake of glancing up, and her gaze was momentarily trapped by the disparaging twist of his wide mouth. Kilo Alpha was obviously not a believer in the arcane arts.

Stubbornness came to her aid. She closed her eyes and dredged up every scrap of information she'd ever read about the relative shape of his hand. "Communication. Air people are communicators, with a strong need to be free. They have an innate distrust of the emotions. They require order..."

With an unsteady forefinger she touched his long, evenly balanced thumb as she tried to force her mind to an order of its own. It was hopeless. "Theories, problems, working out solutions, unraveling mysteries—those are the things you do best. You perceive nature as something to be understood and utilized." Where were the words coming from? Surely her memory wasn't all that good.

As her spate of knowledge evaporated, Shea lifted her eyes to the shadowed face across the tiny round table. The noisy crush of the crowded room seemed to recede until she was aware of nothing except this man, the blazing intensity of his golden eyes, the force of his personality. Was he always this angry, or was it just because she'd been staying in his house?

"Look, I can explain—"

"Is that all?" he interrupted. "No female equivalent of a tall, dark stranger, no long journey with a treasure waiting to be discovered? You don't give a whole lot for your money, do you?"

Stung by his sarcasm, Shea broke away from his gaze and tightened her grip on his hand. All right, so she'd play it his way and pretend she was just a fortune-teller instead of an interloper who owed him the courtesy of an explanation at the very least. "You have the reputation of being a loner," she said softly, in her best "mysterious" tone. "That's not entirely true. It's just that your sights are set above those of most people, and you're too proud to lower them." Had she said that? That wasn't what she'd started out to say.

There it was again, that current, that odd knowing, as though her mind had switched over to automatic pilot. "You should learn to trust," she said quietly, fighting against the compelling energy that seemed focused in the few square inches where their flesh touched. "Just because you have something to hide . . . something . . . behind something else—" She broke off, confused by the words she'd just spoken, words that seemed to have nothing at all to do with the hand she held.

Dave felt the sweat break out on his forehead, saw it bead the surface of his callused hand. God, sweaty palms! He hadn't suffered that ignominy since he was fourteen. Why now?

"How much did they tell you?" he demanded.

"How much did who tell me? About what?"

The four-letter word made Shea flinch, but it never occurred to her to release his hand. "If you mean Jean, she told me you'd broken your leg, but not how you did it. She said you had a rotten disposition. 'A crocodile with a toothache' was the way she put it, if I remember correctly."

She lifted her eyes, hoping to find a glimmer of amusement in his. Anything to defuse the explosive tension. This was more awkward than she'd expected, and she'd hardly expected it to be easy.

"That much you could see for yourself," Dave muttered, still not satisfied that the two of them hadn't set him up. "So go ahead, tell me about the female equivalent of a tall, dark, mysterious stranger who's coming into my life. Or do I have to cross your palm with silver first?" His head lifted disparagingly so that he was able to look down his thrusting, slightly arched nose at her. "Don't tell me the rates have gone up. Shall I tickle your palm with paper, then?"

Shea had an extremely high boiling point. It was possible that Kilo Alpha Four, Zulu Delta Echo just might shove her over the top. "According to your thumb," she went in an unnaturally sweet tone of voice, "you have an enormous store of emotional energy, you're stubborn as a drunken

mule and your own ego is your favorite companion." She
jabbed a freshly polished nail at his index finger. "Your
Jupiter finger shows an overweening pride and a keen power
of observation."

She jabbed again. "Saturn. You have an overgrown sense
of responsibility, one that you'd probably be happier without, and a tendency to brood."

"I have not!"

"Shut up! You asked for this. You're going to get it!"
Shea couldn't believe she'd actually said that. Never in her
life had she told another person to shut up.

She scowled until her heavily mascaraed lashes began to
tangle, and then she went on. "Your finger of Apollo indicates that you're emotionally secure, but—"

"But? Go on, I find all this claptrap fascinating."

Shea's lips tightened. Every raw nerve registered his
skepticism. Before she relinquished his hand, she tilted it
and stared at the line on the edge of the palm, just below the
finger of Mercury. There was only one, as on her own hand.
And as on hers, it was deep and straight and strong.

"What are you looking at now?"

On the verge of telling him that he'd have only one love
but that it would be deep and true and lasting, she swallowed hard and lunged for another topic. "Your girdle of
Venus indicates—"

"My what?" He snatched back his hand and stared at it
suspiciously.

"Your girdle of Venus," Shea repeated, turning her own
palm faceup and pointing to the small, curving line that
looped beneath the two middle fingers. "This one."

Oh, heavens, why hadn't she stuck to something safe and
noncontroversial? If there was such a thing! She tried to
think of a tactful way to describe the passionate nature re-
vealed by the presence and the quality of such a line, and felt

her throat tighten up. Good Lord, how could she even think of sitting here and calmly discussing the man's sex life with him? With a complex, contradictory hand like his—the strength, the energy, both physical and emotional, the inbred reticence, so like her grandfather's—plus those other restraining factors she'd noted, the man was a walking time bomb!

For what seemed like an eternity neither of them moved. Shea's eyes were glued to the knotted fist he nursed in the palm of his other hand. She could feel his eyes on her, but she couldn't have met them if her life depended on it. It was as if she were paralyzed.

"How much do I owe you, Madame Blueskies?" The name was a sneer on his lips.

"Please," she said, agonized.

"Then Jean paid you for the night?"

"It's all taken care of." Let him think what he would, as long as he gave her a moment to recover. Hadn't Jean gotten around to telling him who she was?

"Then you're a party favor, like those idiot hats and noisemakers. Speaking of which, brace yourself, they'll be going off any minute now."

As the odd tension that she alone seemed aware of began to lessen, Shea managed a weak smile. "Then let me be the first to wish you a Happy New Year."

Three

___

When it came it was even worse than she could have imagined. Pete wedged his way through the horn-blowing, embracing couples with two glasses of champagne.

"All finished up, Shea? Been hearing terrific stuff about all those fortunes you told. Here, have a glass of champagne."

Shea took the drink and looked for a place to set it. She'd have preferred something to eat. "Oh, well, they weren't exactly fortunes. You see, palmistry is more a—"

Pete Cummings, half-tight and grinning broadly, ignored her to raise his own glass to his brother-in-law. "What do you think of your little house-sitter? Hidden talents, huh?"

Dave turned a blank look on Shea, who felt a horrid, ingratiating smile begin to take shape on her face.

"You?"

She nodded. "I thought Jean had told you."

"You?" he repeated, glowering thunderously at first Shea, then at poor, mystified Pete. "Dammit, Pete, Jean's gone too far this time. If I get home and find one thing out of line, you'll need the whole damned attorney general's office to get that wife of yours off the hook!"

"She was your sister before she was my wife," Pete said, grinning foolishly.

"Oh, but I've just been sort of camping out until—" Shea put in.

Dave turned on her, hampered only slightly by the crutch he'd jammed under his arm when he'd stood up. "You and who else? Are you working alone, or am I going to have to throw a whole pack of you off my property?"

"A whole pack?" Shea had risen when Pete had joined them, too. Now, as he disappeared into the crowd, she braced herself to do battle. "Now just a minute, you—"

"No, just a minute you," David Pendleton snarled. "I don't know what cock-and-bull story you handed my sister, but it won't work on me. Housekeepers, fortune-tellers— Jean will fall for any sucker line! You stay put right here, you little grifter. I'm going to find one of the boys to drive me home, and you're coming with me."

"Now just a minute," Shea began again. The guilt she'd managed to shove out of sight over the past few days suddenly rose up to mix with her indignation, making her angrier still. "You were angry before you even knew who I was, and I want to know why."

"I was not angry I was fighting mad. It just so happens that I've got a broken leg, I've had a hell of a rough week and then I get dragged to a party to meet some woman before I can even go home. And as if that's not enough, I discover that my meddling sister has turned my house into a home for gypsy fortune-tellers!"

"When Jean said you had the disposition of a crocodile with a toothache she was being kind!"

At six foot two, David Pendleton easily towered over her. The dark slash of his brows tilted ominously toward his jutting nose as he deliberately used his physical superiority to intimidate.

Shea felt behind her for the tiny piecrust table, gasping when it slid away from her fingers. She didn't honestly know whether she'd intended to lean on it or hit him with it. "You'll find nothing out of order, I promise you that. And believe me, if I hadn't left my bags there, nothing on earth would induce me to go back."

Dave simmered under a confusion of warring emotions. Her eyes were so loaded with gunk that it was impossible to determine their color. Black or dark brown, they were snapping like firecrackers. Above a chin that struck him as oddly defenseless, her lips quivered, and he swore under his breath.

"I beg your pardon?" Shea murmured politely, as though her nails weren't drilling holes in the palms of her hands.

Dave eased his weight off his crutch and leaned back against the wall, knowing that Jean would find him soon enough. "I said, what a way to start the New Year," he retorted tiredly.

"Hey, what's going on?" Jean greeted them brightly, turning from one to the other like a cat watching two mice at once. "Shea, come eat before all the good stuff gets gobbled up. I didn't mean for you to work all night on an empty stomach."

Food! Was that what was wrong with her? Was that what caused this hollow feeling that had her practically clinging to the draperies for support? Shea moved swiftly to stand beside the older woman, recognizing salvation when she saw it.

"Pete says he told you about our arrangement, Dave. Neat, huh?" Jean lifted her empty glass in a mock toast to both of them, a smug look on her face. "By the way, how'd you like Connie James?"

"Who the devil is Connie James?"

Shea began to edge away, needing nothing so much as a bit of fresh air and a chance to settle her ruffled nerves. Mike hadn't exaggerated the size of the party. There had to be at least a hundred people in the Cummingses' living room, all of them laughing and talking at once.

"I told you I'd invited someone for you," Shea heard Jean hiss loudly. "She's the redhead in the blue sequined sweater. I tried to introduce you earlier, but you faded away right before my very eyes."

"You expect me to stand around swapping small talk with some overdressed tart when I've just found out you've turned my house over to a tribe of gypsy fortune-tellers? What the hell are you trying to do to me, Jean? Are you still sore because the old man left me the property and you the investments?"

"Hush!" Jean whispered furiously. "Do you want her to hear you?"

"Who, your painted pal in the turban? She's already beat a strategic retreat. Better bar the exits." Shea, trapped in a crush of celebrants only a few feet away, cringed as she heard his rough-edged voice add, "I want her out of there, Jean. And I mean *now*."

"All right, all right," Jean placated as Shea dodged under a glen-plaid arm only to run into a gray flannel shoulder. "She can stay here, only the good Lord knows where I'm going to put her, with Biff's girlfriend sleeping in the corner room and her kid brother bedded down on the trundle in Mike's room. She invited him to come for the rest of the holidays, can you believe it? We never even met the girl before and now she's bringing in her family.''

Shea finally managed to break through the traffic jam and reach the dubious sanctuary of the kitchen. She tossed an anxious glance over her shoulder, but neither Jean's graying page boy nor her brother's thick crop of dark-blond hair was visible. For the moment, at least, she was safe.

From his vantage point, Dave watched the lopsided turban bob across the room, its progress hampered again and again. "Serves you right," he replied, a spark of brotherly malice still evident in his tone. "I always warned you that one day you'd regret turning this place into a panhandler's sanctuary. Remember that out-of-work violinist you took in, the one who made off with all Pete's suits and the better part of a country ham?"

His eyes returned to the last place he'd seen the distinctive headgear. He wasn't finished with Madame Blueskies, not yet. He finally caught sight of her in the kitchen, probably filling her pockets with everything edible or pawnable. Come to think of it, she did have a hungry look about her.

"Well, I still think you owe her something," Jean persisted. "After all, she came all this way just to deliver your stinking old letter."

"Whose letter? What letter?" A neighbor sidled through the milling throng to ask where Jean kept the Pepto Bismol, and Dave waited, patience strained past the breaking point. Aside from the perennial inconvenience of lugging all this damned plaster around with him, his head was beginning to ache. "I hope you didn't leave any valuables lying around in the kitchen."

"Valuables?"

"Your little fortune-teller's out there unattended. What possessed you to set her up in my place, Jean? Wasn't that light-fingered housekeeper you sent me enough?"

"David, just what did Pete tell you, anyway?"

"Verbatim? From the time he picked me up at the airport, I learned more than I really wanted to know about how much it was costing to keep Biff at Carolina, how long it took Pete to document every business mile he drove, how much some dentist in Cabarrus County was paying for imported plastic teeth and how much he was getting for them on a per-mouth basis."

"All right, all right," Jean broke in, knowing her husband's propensity to rattle on while he was driving. Pete's work as an investigator of dental fraud meant that he spent a good part of his time on the road. "About Shea. What did he tell you about Shea Bellwood?"

"'Bellwood'?" Dave scowled, wishing the din would let up so he could hear himself think. "Did you say Bellwood? This Madame Blueskies of yours is named Bellwood?"

Jean groaned. "I should have known better than to trust Pete to relay any message that didn't have to do with bridgework or basketball." So it had been one of her less brilliant ideas. Knowing what a terribly private person her brother was, she should have known better, but it was too late now. "Didn't he even mention the letter?"

"What letter? For cripes' sake, doesn't that stereo in there have a volume control?"

"That's not the stereo. There's this group from high school. The drummer is Chan's girlfriend's brother."

"What do they call themselves, the Sonic Booms?"

"Hey, that's not bad. We've been trying to come up with a catchy name, but most of them—"

"If you're trying to distract me, Jean, it won't work. Dammit, haven't you even been out there since you turned the place over to your friend, Blueskies?"

Jean hung on to the last vestiges of her receding patience. There were times when her baby brother was even more exasperating than her own brood of hellions, and that was saying a lot! "Look, do you have any idea how much time it was taking me to drive all the way out to the hall and get that old mutt off her duff? I had to walk her until she did her business, and that took forever! Did it ever occur to you that I don't have forever?"

"If I get home and discover that little witch has hung her shingle on my entrance gates and started raking in the suckers, she won't have much of a forever, either, I promise you. Oh, hell," he said, tired of the whole wrangle, "Jean, call me a cab, will you? No point in Pete's courting a DWI."

"You're not going to make Shea go home with you?" Jean said anxiously.

"Damned right she's going home with me. Before I let her out of my sight, we're going to take inventory, and if that offends your sense of Southern hospitality, that's tough. Next time maybe you'll think twice before you install one of your strays in my bed."

In the end it was Shea who drove them back out to Pendle Hall. The few cabs in town had all seemingly disappeared, as had the three eldest Cummings boys. Shea couldn't blame them. Given the chance, she'd have disappeared herself.

They borrowed Jean's truck, and Shea promised to return it the next day.

"You're sure you can drive this thing?" Dave asked suspiciously as he watched her lift her shirts and grab the steering wheel to hoist herself inside the cab.

To his irritation, Dave found himself noticing things about her that he'd missed before. Her size, for one thing. She couldn't be more than five foot four, with a hollow-boned sort of frailty that reminded him of one of the smaller shore birds. He had no idea what color her hair was under all those garish rags—or if she even had any. Layers of paint obscured her features, yet there was something about her that continued to draw his eyes, to pluck at his mind with worrisome fingers. "If you can't handle it, say so," he growled, sounding more harsh than he intended.

"I can handle it. I've driven a Jeep over worse roads than you'll ever see."

"I doubt that," he muttered.

Bellwood. Shea Bellwood? Wasn't that the name of Ed Bellwood's little granddaughter? Ed was gone now. He'd just assumed that the kid had gone back to her parents.

Oh, what the hell. He'd sort it out once they got away from this infernal din. Why Jean insisted on inflicting these annual brawls on everybody was a mystery to him. The more the merrier—that had always been her slogan.

Shea took grim pleasure in watching him maneuver his cast awkwardly into the confined space. She refrained from telling him that her driver's license was a Mexican one that might or might not be acceptable in this state. At least she was stone-cold sober. That should weigh in her favor of New Year's Eve in case they got stopped.

Sooner or later she'd have to see about getting herself some form of transportation. Time enough then to update her credentials. After all the red tape she'd gone through with immigration and customs, she could stand to wait a few days before tackling another government agency.

"Take a right," Dave ordered when 133 dead-ended at 211. It was the first time either of them had spoken since they'd left the party.

Tension clamped the muscles at the base of Shea's skull. If this was the way he wanted it, that was fine with her. He was every bit as bad as Jean had described him. What made matters even worse was the aura of raw masculine sensuality that surrounded him, the last thing in the world Shea had been prepared for. It had the effect of compounding an already explosive situation.

"Take a left and then another left when we pick up 133 again."

"I know the way," Shea snapped, resenting everything about the man. "Happy New Year to you, too!"

He grunted expressively, and Shea's small burst of sarcasm seemed to echo endlessly in the metallic silence.

Side streets thinned out. They passed several acres scraped bare of all but a few straggling pines and a dozen neatly aligned mobile homes. Christmas lights still gleamed brightly in an occasional window, and Shea knew a feeling of overwhelming desolation. With her grandfather gone, her mother in Paris and her father remarried and living somewhere in the Midwest, she had no one to fall back on if she ran into trouble.

Not that she would, of course, but all the same, it was a scary feeling.

In the dim glow from the dashboard, Shea was aware of David's eyes on her profile. She gripped the wheel and shifted herself forward on the seat. In her mind's eye, a vision of strong, angular features arose—a blade of a nose that jutted from high, flat cheekbones. His hair wasn't as dark as her own, but darker than blond. His eyes, under slashing brows, were fiercely, blisteringly angry, with a smoldering look of accusation that made her feel irrationally guilty.

What had she done that was so terrible? She'd helped out a friend in an emergency, that was all. She'd fed and walked a dog, brought in mail and papers, dressed up in a tacky costume and filled in for a sick fortune-teller, all to return a simple favor.

And now she was taking this ingrate home, even though it meant that she'd have to drive all the way back to town.

At the rate she was going, it would be morning before she finally got herself a room for the night. Jean had insisted halfheartedly that she go back out to Oak Island, but it was obvious there was no room for her there. Besides, Shea had had enough. She felt like a bone being fought over by two dogs, neither of whom really wanted it.

Dave shifted his leg, cursing as the door handle dug into his back.

"How did you break it?" Shea asked, determined to carry off this whole crazy business with as good grace as possible. She'd invested too much time, money and effort in it to end on such a sour note.

"Kicking strangers off my property," came the disgruntled reply. Actually, he'd been repairing storm damage to one of his antennae and lost his footing, but what difference did it make? He shrugged and stared at the ghostly white pillars that flanked the entrance to his property.

Lips tightening at the rebuff, Shea swerved off onto the poorly maintained driveway without slackening speed, deliberately jolting over the eroded edge of the pavement. She hit every fallen branch and every gully head on, instead of angling to reduce the shock. Not until they pulled up before the house and she switched off the engine did she turn to look at him, and then she wished she hadn't.

Oh, Lord, she was as bad as he was. She'd acted out of pure spite, deliberately using her brief advantage to gain a measure of revenge. The acrid taste of an apology was already on her tongue when Dave thrust open his door. In the harsh light his lean face was pallid under a sheen of perspiration.

"I'm sorry. I could have taken it easier."

The baleful look he sent her spoke more clearly than any words. Grasping the overhead doorframe, he swung himself out of the cab and reached into the back for his crutch.

"Can I help you?" He was tired, she reminded herself. She was tired, too, yet she could understand why he might resent an interloper.

"You can unlock the door, if it's not asking too much."

Shea darted ahead and fumbled for the key Jean had given her. She'd return it when she did the truck and then get someone to drive her back to the motel. She'd already decided on a place to stay. It was centrally located and would give her a base of operations until she could think beyond the immediate future.

From the back of the house came a joyous yelp, and Shea tossed her purse at a chair and hurried toward the kitchen, glad of an excuse to escape. She hadn't missed Dave's quick survey of the living room. What had he expected to find, for goodness' sake, the whole house stripped bare? Graffiti on the French wallpaper? Initials carved in the fruitwood paneling?

The swinging door fanned noisily behind her as she knelt beside the wicker dog bed. "He's finally home, and you know it, don't you, old darling?" She scratched the special place at the lower end of the old dog's back, but Lady's hazy brown eyes were focused in mute adoration at the doorway. Shea heard David's distinctive footsteps coming toward the kitchen. The door fanned again, and then he was behind her, so close she could feel his cast brushing against her skirt.

The dog was writhing with excitement. Shea stood and made room for the two of them to get together. It was obvious that her presence wouldn't be missed. Dave pulled up a kitchen chair and opened his arms, accepting Lady's lavishly given kisses and scratching the place Shea had discovered on her own. The soft murmur that followed her as she headed for the stairway came as something of a surprise. Not the shelty's keening attempts to communicate, but the other, deeper voice. Who would have suspected such an abrasive baritone could sound so tender.

A shiver overtook her, leaving a rash of goose bumps down both thighs. She wasn't cold, just somehow... empty?

Once in her room, Shea unwound the turban and placed it in one of the open suitcases. She'd get a dog of her own, she decided as she began removing layers of pendants and beads, bangles and rings. She unhooked the gaudy star-and-half-moon earrings she'd bought when she'd first had her ears pierced. She'd been fourteen then, and she'd thought them perfectly beautiful.

Well, it was over now. She was finally free of the past. Or as free as anyone can ever be, considering the emotional baggage one carries through life.

She lay across one suitcase and forced the latch closed. It weighed a ton, even though she'd distributed the Bellwood silver, her jewelry supplies and her hand tools among items of clothing. She should probably have sold the silver. Practical to the end, her grandfather had suggested it before his last heart attack, but Shea had never even considered it. She had little enough family heritage. A few strands of beads and the complete set of sterling that had been Bellwood property for four generations gave her a feeling of security that no amount of money could supply.

She buckled the strap around the lumpy girth—the key had long since been lost, but the luggage was indestructible. Shoving it through the door, she left it at the top of the stairs and set about shedding her Madame Blueskies image.

The murmur of a deep voice drifted up the stairway, and Shea smiled in spite of her tiredness. She saw herself putting the mismatched china in to wash while her grandfather warmed up the radio receiver for the evening session, hearing again the screeches, whines and the rattle of code that had been music to her grandfather's ears. She'd never gotten hooked on amateur radio, but those distant, unknown voices had been a part of her life, filling their small house each evening.

"This is KA4ZDE, that's Kilo Alpha four, Zulu Delta Echo, overlooking the Cape Fear River and running barefoot on a three-element yagi." That had been her earliest recollection of the man she had come so far to see.

Before she'd learned that a "three-element yagi" was an antenna and "running barefoot" meant operating without a linear amplifier, her mind had painted wild pictures of a man in a loincloth running barefoot on a narrow, swinging bridge over a raging river.

Now, lathering her face in an effort to remove the heavy pancake makeup Jean had insisted she wear, Shea smiled in remembrance. David Pendleton in loincloth and cast was about as wild a vision as the law allowed.

Her smile faded, and she scrubbed vigorously to remove the last traces of the magenta stains from her lips. Granted that the man was tired and out of sorts, he still had no right to be so caustic. He hadn't even given her a chance to explain about the letter.

Peeled down to her colorful skirt and plain navy top, Shea felt considerably better. She slathered moisturizer on her face, touched her lips with a peach-tinted gloss and exchanged her huaraches for a pair of navy flats. Better still. She tousled her hair and let its glossy weight slither through her fingers, then tackled the job of packing the jewelry she'd worn into the second suitcase.

She was tucking in the last of roll of hammered-silver-and-filigree beads when she heard the sound of breaking glass, followed by a solid stream of profanity. Her first instinct was to hurry down to see what had happened.

It was none of her business, she reminded herself with a growing sense of freedom. Let him break every dish in the house. It was his house; they were his dishes. It wasn't up to her to do anything for anyone.

It occurred to Shea that there was surprisingly little satisfaction in that particular observation. Sitting on the suitcase, she latched it, belted it and shoved it out to sit beside its mate. She had just managed to get the first one down the stairs, when the kitchen door swung open and David braced himself in the opening. "Would you mind telling me what in Sam Hill you did to my dog?"

Shea's eyes widened at the sight of the bloody towel wrapped around his left hand. She deliberately refrained from mentioning it. "The only thing I did to your dog was feed her and pet her and take her for walks."

"Lady doesn't take to strangers. Now you've got her all upset."

"She took to me, and what do you mean, *I've* got her all upset?"

"She won't eat her mash. Keeps trying to get into the refrigerator."

"Did you put warm milk on it?" If he was trying to win her sympathy with his bloody hand and his broken leg he was out of luck. Shea averted her eyes from the gory towel, but it was impossible not to notice the stance that thrust his hips aggressively forward. Those corduroys had seen better days. Aside from being slit to accommodate his cast, they had been worn practically threadbare.

"Lady doesn't drink milk," he informed her disparagingly. "If you knew anything at all about dogs you'd know they can't digest it."

Shea placed her hands on her hips in an unconscious effort to match his aggressiveness and go him one better. "Oh? I guess you forgot to mention that to Lady. She's been lapping it up all week, and I haven't seen a sign of her not being able to handle it. And believe me, I'd have noticed."

Dave's darkening gaze moved past her to the lumpy suitcase in the middle of the room. It was the soft-sided kind, and it was all but bursting at the seams. Launching himself away from the doorway, he limped across and nudged it with his cast. The metallic jangle was clearly audible.

"Would you mind opening that?" he drawled, gesturing insolently with the tip of his crutch.

She could have killed him. She was tempted to snatch his crutch and trip him with it. "Yes, I would mind." Snatching up the handle, she struggled to lift the bag off the floor. Oh, Lord, if she ever found a place to light she'd never budge again! She was sick of traveling, sick of hauling everything she owned wherever she went and having to unpack over and over again for airport security and customs officials.

"If you think you're walking out of here with that you're nuts, gypsy. Eight generations of Pendletons have used that silverware, and I'm not about to see it end up in some sleezy pawn shop."

"Look at it this way," Shea said sweetly, "you'll never have to polish it again."

"I didn't have to polish it before, but that doesn't mean I'm going to hand it over to you." Dave's eyes narrowed. There was something different about her. She'd taken off that outlandish hat, for one thing, but it was more than that. Whatever it was, he was in no mood to ease up on her, Bellwood or no Bellwood. He knew all about her background—if that's who she was. Probably teamed up with her mother the minute poor Ed died.

"Are you going to open it, or shall I do it for you?" He was hurting, and dammit, he hadn't needed this aggravation.

With her left arm being pulled from its socket, Shea wondered if needling him was worth the effort. "I haven't touched your precious silver," she informed him tiredly. "And I didn't have time to launder the linens I used, so you'll probably want to incinerate them."

The letter. After all that had happened, she'd almost forgotten that blasted letter!

Dropping the bag with a dangerous disregard for the few fragile items inside, Shea fumbled with her purse. Before she could extract the rumpled envelope she'd brought so far, Dave dropped his crutch and, with a swiftness that belied his handicapped state, attacked her suitcase.

There was no other word to describe it. Those hands she'd studied such a short while ago ripped off the strap, unfastened the latch, and before she could stop him, he was drawing out the nightgown in which she'd rolled her grandmother's sterling berry spoon.

"What the—" he exclaimed, looking startled as the heavy, gleaming service piece hit the floor.

"Would you mind?" Furious, she knelt beside him, tugging at his arms.

A slip came out next. It was her oldest one, a soft white cotton. The one with the broken strap. Out tumbled a silver-and-amber pendant and two salad forks.

"David—Mr. Pendleton, please..."

Hopelessly Shea sat back on her heels and watched, knowing that nothing she could say would stop him now. For some reason this madman had it in for her. He was convinced she'd cleaned him out—probably because of the housekeeper Jean had mentioned.

Ironically, she'd told him he should learn to take things at face value. Pity he hadn't listened. "That's my family silver, in case you're interested," she informed him.

"Yeah, sure it is. I always travel with my own silverware, too."

Shea closed her eyes when he started on her underpants. They were plain white cotton, certainly nothing to be ashamed of, but seeing those strong, dark hands unrolling them, then removing the burnisher, the ring mandrel and the packet of saw blades was almost more than she could take.

Especially in the early hours of the morning.

The man was a fiend. How could he possibly accuse her of stealing those tools? No one but a jeweler would even own such things, and he was no jeweler.

"Are you satisfied?" she demanded when the carefully packed contents of her suitcase were reduced to three untidy piles—one of underwear, one of silverware and jewelry and one of hand tools.

"Interesting. No plastic explosives for blowing safes? Or isn't that your style. You're a specialist, is that it? You case your victims with the fortune-telling scam and then move in on them, right? Clever."

He sounded as disgusted as he looked, and Shea fought back a primitive urge to wipe that superior sneer off this face. *Stay calm, don't raise your voice—it can all be cleared up with a simple explanation.*

"Well? Come on, Madame Blueskies, you had plenty to say earlier."

Shea began cramming her belongings back into her suitcase, not taking the time to wrap the carefully polished silver. So she'd spend a few days pumicing away scratches—the important thing was to get away from here before she did something truly unforgivable. She would not descend to her parents' level and solve things by seeing who could yell loudest.

While Dave sat on the floor watching her every move, Shea stuffed in the last of her garments. Primly she seated herself on the closed case and reached between her ankles to fasten the latch. That done, she headed for the stairway and brought down her other piece of luggage.

Only then did she look directly at him. "If you find anything missing or anything out of place, I can be reached at the Waterfront Motel in Southport for the next few days. This—" she fumbled inside her purse and extracted the dog-eared envelope she'd carried almost two thousand miles "—this is from my grandfather. Keep in mind that he wasn't well when he wrote it. He died not long afterward. If it's any comfort to you, I don't think he could have known what a miserable excuse for a human being you turned out to be."

From his position on the floor, Dave stared at the letter and then at the woman who'd handed it to him. She looked young and tired and incredibly proud. And she was looking down at him as if he were something unpleasant on the sole of her shoe.

"What is this?" he muttered, growing increasingly embarrassed. "Your grandfather?"

"Edward Bellwood." For good measure, Shea repeated her grandfather's call sign, taking grim pleasure in the look of uncertainty that replaced the angry scowl on David Pendleton's face. "He insisted that I deliver it to you personally, and I can tell you this—it hasn't been any picnic. If I'd known what sort of person you were, I'd have dropped the thing into the nearest mailbox. Minus the stamp!"

Grabbing on to the newel, Dave swung himself to his feet, cursing as the cut on his hand opened up again and started to bleed. "Look, if I was out of line tonight—" he began tentatively, gesturing a vague apology with the envelope.

Shea, eyes glinting with indignation, kept her voice under admirable control. "Oh, you weren't out of line. You were absolutely right about me. I've robbed you blind and alienated your dog and taken advantage of your sister, and—and..."

Oh, God, she was going to cry. Anger, pure, white-hot rage, rose up to choke her, to burn her eyes. Snatching blindly at her suitcases, she managed to get them both out the door before he could stop her. Fortunately, she'd pulled the truck up as close to the house as possible. The bags would have to go in front—she could never manage to lift them into the back.

A crutch and a grimy cast entered her field of vision as she bent to lift the first one. "I'll put that in the truck for you."

"I can handle it," she said stiffly.

"You obviously can't," Dave snapped. "Look, maybe we'd better talk."

"Would you please move?"

Behind her, the eight-day clock on the mantel cleared its throat and dinged once, which told her nothing at all except that it was half-past something. Shea found the truck door blocked by the formidable bulk of plaster and corduroy, topped by a solid wall of chest. Her eyes were still burning—from all the junk she'd smeared on them, no doubt—and she jutted her chin to make up for the temporary weakness.

"I've managed to get myself and both bags from Tuxtla Guiterrez to Pendle Hall. I can certainly manage to get from here to Southport."

Dave grunted something unintelligible, and then he found himself unexpectedly trapped in the depths of a pair of navy eyes. He'd never seen blue eyes so dark before, or quite so disapproving. "Look, this is crazy." He gestured impatiently with his towel-draped hand. "If you've come all the way from Mexico for my sake—"

"I didn't." The urge to cry had left her, thank goodness. Now if only she could get rid of the urge to kick his good leg out from under him. "I came for the sake of my grandfather. For some reason it seemed important to him that I deliver this letter in person."

Dave patted the pocket he'd shoved the letter in. He'd read it later. Right now he felt an urgency of another sort, one he neither understood nor welcomed. "Thank you."

Shea nodded. "You're welcome. And now if you'll excuse me, I'll—"

She stepped back, shaken by a restless energy that seemed to crackle the air around them. It was his fault she was beginning to fall apart. It had been a long, exhausting day, and he'd never even given her a chance to explain. Worse still, he hadn't been at all what she'd been expecting. Not at all. She was just too tired to cope with anything more tonight.

Leaning on his crutch, Dave watched her drive off. Whoever she turned out to be, he ought to be damned glad to see the last of her. But with his head pounding, his cast itching and a fresh cut on his hand—thanks to his own clumsy impatience—he was certain of only two things: he hadn't seen the last of her, and it wasn't exactly joy he was feeling as he watched the taillights disappear into the night.

Four

—

Leaning his naked back against the crumpled pillow, Dave read the letter for the third time. A shipping invoice, that was about the size of it. God knows he owed the old man one, but to have her land on his doorstep this way, with no warning... Well, it was awkward, to say the least.

Shea Bellwood. He'd thought—if he'd thought about her at all—that she was still a child. Ed had mentioned her now and then when she'd first come to live with him, but for the most part they'd stuck to more impersonal matters. Radio was, after all, a pretty public means of conversing. When the old man had died, he'd sort of figured the kid had gone back to whichever one of her parents could take her.

But that was no child he'd insulted, threatened and virtually kicked out of the house. Under all those layers of paint she'd looked older. Without the makeup it was hard to tell. Fifteen? Eighteen? Twenty?

"I'm calling in a favor, son," Ed Bellwood had written. And Dave's mind immediately dived back through the years to the first time he'd met the man who had come to mean so much to him.

He'd been headed for South America on the Pan-American Highway, a spare pair of boots and jeans, a raincoat and damned little else strapped to the back of his Norton. After two months on the road he'd still been unable to shake the feelings of anger and depression that had followed his father's fatal heart attack. He'd about made up his mind to cut across to Villahermosa, on the Gulf Coast Highway, and head for home when it had happened.

Carelessness? Tiredness? He'd never really known. All he remembered afterward was a lot of loose gravel on the pavement as he was coming up on the junction with Mexican 195 at Escopetazo, and braking for a piece of road machinery.

When he awoke, he was in a hospital in Tuxtla, looking up into a pair of worried gray eyes.

"You were outclassed from the start, son. I'd skip the rematch if I were you."

"The bike?" he'd asked, trying to focus his groggy mind.

"I saved her for you. Might take some doing to put her back together, but you'll have plenty of time."

His Norton. His sweet-running, dependable, silent companion. He'd felt like crying, and then he felt guilty as hell, because he could weep for a piece of machinery when he still hadn't wept for his father.

"Anybody you need to contact? I'm a ham operator. I can get a phone patch through to most anywhere, hook you up so you can talk to your folks. Might be a good idea to let 'em know you're all right, son. Be a while before you're writin' any postcards."

That had been his introduction to Edward Bellwood, entomologist and ham-radio operator. The months he'd spent with the crusty old widower in his bungalow in Tuxtla had healed more than his bruised and broken body. He'd finally been able to talk through his grief, his guilt and the anger he still felt for the father who'd been determined to relive his own life through his son.

Nor had it been a one-way street. Ed had talked, too... about the wife who'd died and left him, the son who'd run wild during the sixties, getting mixed up with a woman who was even wilder and producing a child out of wedlock.

Shea.

"And now we're back full circle," Dave said softly as the spidery handwriting blurred before his eyes. Thanks to Ed Bellwood and his deep font of understanding, he'd come to terms with himself over his stormy relationship with his father. He no longer felt guilty, only sad for the man who'd never known how to bend. Dave had had to fight for his choice of a career just as he'd fought for everything else in his life. He'd had his heart set on studying geology; his father had insisted that he study law.

Before he'd left Tuxtla for the States, Dave had been infected with the radio bug. The old man's enthusiasm had been contagious. He'd learned enough from Ed to apply for his novice ticket, and a year later he'd gotten his general license. They'd talked frequently, mostly about their work and their mutual interest, radio. He'd been stunned to learn of the old man's death.

I've done my best for the child, Dave, and now I'm asking you to finish the job for me. See that she gets a decent job and a place to stay. Look after her until she finds a respectable man to marry her. She insisted on studying some arty nonsense. I'd hate to think she'd turn out like her mother.

The last I heard, Mia was in Paris living with a boy half her age. I'd just as soon Shea didn't know where she was. As for my son, he seems to have come to his senses after all these years. He's remarried now, but there's no question of his taking her to live with him and his new family. I hope the child will never know about this. She's been hurt enough.

Shea's a good girl and a hard worker, but inclined to be impulsive. I might have protected her too much, but seeing that she wasn't mine, I felt I had to. She'll do all right once she's had time to get her bearings, but I don't want her to try to find either of her parents. Keep an eye on her, will you, Dave? I don't ask more than that. There's no one else I can turn to for help.

P.S. Delivering this letter was the only way I could think of to get her there. Don't tell her about it. She might not understand.

It was almost nine when Shea woke up on the first day of January. It took several minutes for her to realize where she was. As the impersonal furniture of the motel room came into focus she yawned. So far, so good. Not exactly palatial, but it would do for now. At least the view was superb.

She'd finally delivered the letter. As of this minute, this day, she was on her own. All in all, it wasn't a bad beginning for a new year. Now that she'd fulfilled her obligations, she might even make a few resolutions.

Resolution number one: find the nearest restaurant and order the biggest breakfast they offered.

She was finishing her third cup of coffee, when Dave came into the restaurant next to the motel. Even with the glare of morning sunlight in her eyes, there was no mistaking that silhouette. Or the impatient, lurching gait.

"Still here, I see," he observed, bracing himself as he loomed over her.

Shea remained silent. The fact that she was still there had nothing to do with him. Their business was finished. She toyed with her coffee cup, uncomfortably aware of the lean torso on a level with her face. There was a clumsily wound bandage on his left hand, making the dark hairs around it spring into even more prominent relief.

"Mind if I join you?" There was more than a hint of irritation in his tone, and it occurred to Shea that a man like Kilo Alpha would not be accustomed to dismissal. Especially by women.

"Help yourself. There's a little more coffee in the pot." She nodded at the insulated carafe. "You won't mind if I leave you now? I have to return Jean's truck."

"And then what?"

"What do you mean, 'and then what'?" She paused in the act of gathering up her purse and jacket.

"After you deliver the pickup. Is Jean dropping you off somewhere? Or are you moving in on her again?"

Shea bit back a sharp retort. Nevertheless she was forced to consider the question seriously. She'd return the truck to Jean, and then what? Jean would have to bring her back to the motel? Rather like a game of musical chairs. The fact was, she hadn't thought beyond the delivery of that damned letter.

"I'm not prying," Dave explained, looking more embarrassed than Shea would have thought possible. "I was wondering—well, you see, the fact is . . ."

He was so obviously ill at ease that she began to relent. Considering the way they'd parted, that was a minor miracle.

"Look, I know it's none of my business, but do you have a—a job lined up? I mean, are you in a hurry to get to wherever you're going?"

This might even prove entertaining, Shea thought, wondering what had brought about the thaw. "No, I'm in no particular hurry. Did you need a ride? I can wait if you want to have some breakfast first."

Dave shifted his bulk in the small chair. This wasn't going to be easy, any way he handled it. "I don't need breakfast," he said gruffly, marshaling the arguments in favor of her staying on in Southport. There weren't all that many, and none of them was valid. If she'd made up her mind to move on, then there was little he could do about it, short of kidnapping.

"You should never skip breakfast." Shea made an effort to ignore the play of sunlight across those magnificent shoulders. "When your body's been fasting for hours, it needs fuel to function properly."

"Yeah, well, that's what I mean—it's the proper functioning of my body that's worrying me. I managed to get here under my own steam, but I damned near wrecked the Jeep twice on the way into town."

"You drove? In that thing?" Shea leaned over and peered down at the massive cast on his right leg.

"I can bend it, at least. Up until recently I couldn't even do that."

"It's a wonder you didn't get picked up by the highway patrol."

"For what? My foot might have been a little heavy on the accelerator, but not that heavy."

"But you were plastered," she reminded him with a perfectly straight face.

For what seemed an eternity, they stared into each other's eyes. Shea cracked first. A smile quivered on her lips, and then Dave grinned, and suddenly, against all odds, they were friends.

Or at least, if not exactly friends, at least no longer deadly enemies.

"About last night," Dave said awkwardly. "I'm sorry. I was way out of line, and my only excuse is—"

"You don't have to apologize," Shea interjected. "I know you were tired and not in a party mood, and then to have me sprung on you ... Jean told me about that housekeeper she got for you. I should have explained right away, but somehow, things sort of got mixed up."

"You might say," Dave murmured, taking in everything about her, from the healthy gloss of her thick brown hair to the shy warmth of her unusual eyes. Navy. He couldn't recall ever seeing eyes that color before.

"How's your hand?" Shea asked. In trying to escape the compelling intensity of his gaze, she turned to the first topic that came to mind.

"Other than unsightly, it's okay. Amazing how clumsy a man can be trying to juggle a glass, a pitcher and a crutch."

"Was the cut deep?"

"Just a scratch." He glanced down at the untidy wad of gauze and grimaced. "I didn't know how to finish the thing off, so I just kept winding until I ran out of gauze. Slight case of overkill, huh?"

"I thought maybe you were trying to elicit my sympathy."

"Would it have worked?"

"If I'd had a weapon," Shea admitted, "I'd probably have inflicted a few wounds myself. You seem to manage pretty well without my help, though."

"Speaking of managing," Dave said, hunching forward to lean his arms on the table. "I do seem to have a problem you might be able to help me with."

"You want your palm re-read to include the new line?"

He chuckled, remembering his thoughts the night before when Madame Blueskies had rendered her interpretation of his personality. Damned accurate in some respects, come to think of it. "Yeah, why not? Wasn't there some sort of a thirty-day warranty on your work?"

"You get what you pay for," she said dryly.

Shifting his weight, Dave dug into the pocket of his close-fitting jeans and came up with a coin. "Can't vouch for the silver content," he murmured, taking her hand in his and marking an X in her palm. "Now shall we adjourn to your tent and get on with it?"

He paid for her breakfast in spite of her arguments, and Shea followed him outside into the blinding sun. Overhead, scores of gulls swooped and called for scraps. With the wind blowing in off the mouth of Corncake inlet, it wasn't as warm as it had looked from inside the restaurant.

She turned and held out her hand. "Thank you for the breakfast, Dave. I'm glad—since you were Granddad's friend, I mean—that we had a chance to part on better terms. It's a nice way to start the new year."

"Whoa, hold on there. Who said anything about parting? I thought we had it all settled."

She'd forgotten how tall he was, how small she felt standing next to him. Without thinking, she moved around until he was shielding her from the raw wind that cut right through her new jeans. "Settled what? You mean about your palm reading?" She laughed breathlessly, feeling more than a little intimidated by the sheer masculine appeal of the man. "Sorry, Madame Blueskies never works on legal holidays."

"Then I'll just have to see that Madame Blueskies hangs around long enough to make good on her guarantee, won't I?"

Had she mentioned any guarantee? She didn't remember it. Certainly she wouldn't have been fool enough to offer a guarantee, as nervous as she'd been about the whole business.

Taking her by the arm, Dave led her over to the Jeep. She'd driven it only once, on a shopping trip to Southport. "Go on, get in out of the wind before you freeze. Takes a while to get acclimatized, even to our mild winters." He'd led her to the driver's side, and once she was in, he took his place in the passenger seat.

"'Mild'! I'd hate to see what you call 'cold.'" Shea waited for him to shove his crutch along the side and settle himself in the passenger seat. The heat of the sun through the windshield almost offset the draft that found its way through the leaky canopy.

"Okay," she said firmly, taking the bandaged hand he laid across her lap. "You're asking a lot for twenty-five cents, but let's see the damage." Under an inch of gauze she discovered a scratch that angled across the base of his thumb. Some wound! She couldn't believe the fuss a grown man could make over something so insignificant.

She cleared her throat and assumed her best Madame Blueskies tone. "Considering its location on the Mount of Mars—" she touched the protruding pad of flesh between thumb and forefinger "—I'd say it might have an influence, at least for the next few days. This mount has to do with your physical courage—or possibly your temper. Mars was the Roman god of war, and from the mount's development, I'd say you have more than your share."

"Of temper or courage?"

Shea bit back a smile. "Well, certainly of the first. I don't know about your courage, do I?"

"I thought Madame Blueskies was supposed to know all and tell all."

"As a matter of fact, Madame Blueskies has retired. I'm just filling in for her until a permanent replacement can be found." Shea wondered at the catalytic effect this man had on her imagination. Not all of the words that flowed from her tongue came from her conscious mind. Nor did every image that took shape in her head have to do with palmistry.

"What are the madame's immediate plans, if you don't mind my asking?"

Shea restored the hand she'd been holding to its owner's lap. In a case where clear thinking was called for, she didn't need that distraction. Just sitting here beside him was distraction enough. "The madame is planning on taking a few days' much-needed vacation, first of all. After that, who knows?"

Dave studied his companion thoughtfully. He could push the matter through, or he could let it drop. He'd come after her. He'd tried. How far did his obligation extend?

"And how is madame fixed for transportation?"

"Transportation? You mean right now?"

"How are you planning to get around during this vacation of yours, Shea? Bus? Taxi? Rental?"

"Oh. That kind of transportation," she said, embarrassed to admit that she'd hadn't thought beyond delivering the letter. And there'd hardly been time since. "A bicycle, probably. Is there a place I could rent one?"

"Weather might be a problem, but if it's a bicycle you want, Jean probably has a garageful. Can you ride a boy's bike?"

It had been years since she'd ridden a bike of any sort, but she nodded. "Sure. Anything will be fine. I might look around at used cars, but I don't want to rush into anything."

"Good policy." Dave watched her slender, surprisingly callused fingers systematically unravel the edge of his straw seat mat. He'd needed a new one, anyhow. "Meanwhile, what would you say to swapping a few hours of chauffeuring for the use of the Jeep?"

"You mean chauffeuring you?"

He shrugged. It would do as a means of keeping her around until he could be sure she was going to be all right. And if it happened to serve his own needs, so much the better.

A phone call brought Mike and Chan to collect the truck, and in the small waterfront park next to the restaurant, the four of them discussed the situation. The boys were plainly relieved to have escaped chauffeuring duties.

"You were the hit of the party, Shea. If you need a manager, I'm your man."

"Hey, Shea, I hope you're a good driver. Remember, don't ride the clutch, don't swing wide on the turns, come to a complete stop at every—"

"Don't I hear your mother calling you, boys?" Dave put in irritably.

"Sure, sure, we can take a hint." Laughing, the two gangling youths backed away, stuffing potato chips and tossing every third one to the clamoring gulls that circled overhead. "Don't let him scare you, Shea. Just be sure you're out of reach of that stick of his when you cuss him out. He sure can't catch you."

Shea and Dave started with a tour of Oak Island. "Once you get the lay of the land," Dave explained as they passed Jean's wooded street and headed out onto the beach strip, "it's not hard to understand. Oak Island runs east and west, with the Atlantic on one side and the Inland Waterway on the other. On the western tip of the island, Big Davis Canal runs in behind the beach strand, splitting Folly's End and about half of Long Beach away from the residential part of Oak Island."

"Looks like a fat clothespin to me," Shea murmured, peering at the map.

Dave shot her a skeptical look. "At any rate, here's Yaupon Beach, and there's Caswell at the top end, jutting out into Cape Fear Inlet."

"Do I need to remember all this?"

"You'll catch on with practice. I've been winding up some research at Lockwood Folly Inlet, but this thing with the leg sort of put me behind schedule. If you don't mind spending part of your vacation at the beach, we could work out a deal that would suit both our needs."

As he waited for her reply, Shea wondered just how she'd been maneuvered into agreeing to this crazy arrangement. She'd done a few foolish things before on the spur of the moment, to her grandfather's great distress, but this was ridiculous!

As if he sensed the very moment when she conceded, Dave exhaled heavily and leaned back in his seat. "Turn right at the stop sign and keep going all the way to the end."

What had she gotten herself into? She knew nothing at all about the man except that he'd been her grandfather's friend. And he was Jean's brother. And he had a vile temper that could turn on and off at the drop of a hat. At least he'd had the grace to apologize. Some men wouldn't have.

"By the way, you do have a license, don't you?"

"It's Mexican."

"We'll see about getting it changed tomorrow."

The high-pitched hum of the tires was oddly soothing, and Shea began to relax, in spite of her misgivings. With one hand, she pulled the soft pink turtleneck of her sweater up to her chin, stirring a drift of her jasmine scent. This might not be so bad, after all . . . for a temporary job.

Dave shifted restlessly, and his hand brushed against her side. Shea was startled at her immediate physical response, even through her quilted jacket. Was she slated to go through life registering her every emotion this way? Good Lord, her insides couldn't take it!

"Look, Dave, I think I'd better explain that I won't be staying around long enough to drive you much." Another impulse. The impulse to get as far away as quickly as she could.

"You've made plans? I wasn't aware—"

"I know you weren't," Shea said hurriedly. How could he have been? She hadn't been herself. "I'll be looking for a place to settle permanently, and I can't afford to wait too long."

"Do you know yet where you'll be going?" he asked quietly. "By the way, you're doing about ten miles over the speed limit."

Chagrined, she eased off the gas pedal. It wasn't like her to speed. Normally she was extremely conservative in everything she did. Her grandfather had worked hard to get her to control that unfortunate streak of impulsiveness she'd inherited from somewhere, and she'd been grateful to him for it.

"No, I don't know where I'll be going," she said deliberately. All she knew was that this arrangement wasn't going to work. She'd let herself be talked into it. For all she knew, he could be an ax murderer. Even his own sister hadn't had many kind words to say for him.

What did she really know about the man? That he'd let a lovely old home go to ruin, that he didn't go out of his way to be polite, that he jumped to conclusions on the flimsiest of evidence.

Casting a sideway look, she met his eyes head on and glanced hastily away again, gripping the steering wheel until her knuckles whitened. She knew, for instance, that his jeans were split higher than they really needed to be for the sake of a knee-length cast. She knew that he disturbed her in a way no other man had ever done. He was neither classically handsome nor particularly pleasant, but it didn't seem to make any difference.

She'd known—not that she'd admitted it—last night when he'd sat down before her and extended his hand, that his touch affected her the way the blue flame of a blow torch affected some metals, turning them every color of the rainbow and then reducing them to a molten puddle. Something to do with molecular structure, no doubt. Whatever the cause, she could do without the effect.

"Turn off here," he directed, pointing to a broken strip of pavement that veered away from the highway and ended abruptly several hundred feet farther.

Shea looked about curiously. The beach flattened out to a broad expanse of white sand, littered here and there with small gatherings of driftwood and shells. Behind them, the cottages of Long Beach huddled among the dunes.

"Welcome to Folly's End," Dave said, gesturing to the empty beach before them but including the three dilapidated cottages that lined the abandoned spur of road.

"This is it?"

"This is it. What's left of it. Think you can find enough to occupy yourself for half an hour or so while I look around?"

A beach was a beach, and as beaches went, this one was beautiful. Shea was more than content to explore. It was hard to resist the urge to run headlong out across the wide, flat strip of sand. "You mean this is where you work?"

He laughed at that. "Believe it or not, it is. For the time being, at least. Half an hour, all right?"

"Do you need me?" she asked uncertainly. What could he do here? He certainly wasn't very mobile.

"No, I'm fine," he reassured her, reaching for his crutch. "Might as well look around as long as I'm here, see what changes there've been since the last time I was out."

Dave watched her take off, running like a kid without even bothering to look back. What if he'd said, "Hell, yes, I need you." Would she have stayed with him?

And if she had, what could she have done, supported him while he trudged through the sand? Asked a hundred stupid questions, most of which he couldn't have answered? He was better off without her.

Lowering himself carefully, he sat on a shelving bank and watched as she paused to examine a shell. Actually, there was little he could do short of floundering around in the sand. If he was going to fall on his face, he'd prefer to do it without an audience.

Taking a small notebook from his hip pocket, he stared for a while at the surf line, noting the subtle differences in the half-buried row of sandbags since the last time he'd been here. He scribbled a few cryptic notes, then let his gaze sweep around as far as he could see, noting the relative position of the shoals to the posts he'd driven down a week before.

Across Lockwood Folly Inlet, Holden Beach was partially obscured behind a salt haze. He'd have to get over there in the next day or so. Meanwhile, all was quiet on the western front. Or so it seemed. He could go on watching the area a while longer, at least until the book came out. If they'd moved on to another section of the coast, he'd either find an excuse to research another inlet or see if he had a reliable contact nearby.

Something had to be done to stop the flow of drugs. The network of inlets and coastal marshes that were his special area of interest made him a natural to work with the authorities. They were vastly undermanned and underbudgeted for the monumental task of policing the coast. He'd been contacted a few years back, given a thorough security check, and since then, he'd done double duty: completing the research for his second book on erosion patterns along the middle Atlantic and pinpointing drop areas for more than one major drug-smuggling operation.

The trouble was that as soon as one pipeline was traced to the source and put out of business, another one sprang up in its place. This was the first time he'd had to work so close to home, though, and it made him nervous as hell. He was coming to hate the whole business, but as long as he could be useful, he couldn't refuse to help out.

He'd been carrying when he'd wrecked the Norton in Escopetazo. God knows where he'd be now if Ed hadn't been the one to find him. The old man had had the foresight to go through his pockets before he'd taken him to the hospital. Otherwise he'd probably still be rotting in some Mexican jail.

Ed had never said a word. After a while, when they'd gotten to be friends, Ed had talked about his son, about the time Willis Bellwood had dropped out of college to run with a bunch that had been into some pretty heavy stuff. That was as close as the old man had ever come to explaining why he'd destroyed evidence to protect a dumb kid with a king-size chip on his shoulder.

Hell, yes, he owed the old man one. He'd look after his granddaughter if he had to hog-tie her to do it. He had friends in Wilmington. He could probably get one of them to take her on if she had any sort of training at all. Meanwhile, she could make herself useful by carting him around until he got free of this plaster.

Five

By the end of the first week Shea had made up her mind. She'd seen enough of the area to be infected by the easy charm of white frame houses and friendly faces, of shrimp boats and Spanish moss. Besides, she didn't have enough money to travel any great distance, even if she knew of another place to go. Of one thing she was certain: she could never go back to Savannah, where she'd lived with her parents. A new beginning meant just that—building from the ground up, with no remnants of the past to distract her.

Dave might be a distraction of another sort, but she managed to convince herself that he had nothing to do with her decision. She'd simply weighed the pros and cons and come to a logical, practical conclusion.

Each day, according to Dave's instructions, she arrived at Pendle Hall one hour before low tide. Their destination never varied, nor did they stay more than two hours as a rule. Often they dropped by Jean's house for coffee, and once they stayed for an impromptu barbecue. Jean never questioned the fact that Shea had taken on the job as Dave's driver, but now and then, Shea intercepted a speculative look.

"By the way, what was in that letter?" the older woman asked one day as they were clearing away the remains of lunch. She had already done her daily stint and delivered Dave back to Pendle Hall. She'd stopped by to ask Jean for the name of a reliable realtor and stayed for lunch.

"Beats me."

Jean paused in the act of eating leftover potato salad to stare at her. "You mean you never even asked?"

"Considering the way we started out, would you if you'd been me?"

"But you're long past that stage now." Jean quirked a sandy eyebrow. "Aren't you?"

"I'd like to think so, but with your brother, who can tell? Some days he's almost pleasant, other times..." Shea shook her head. "Meanwhile, I've got transportation while I look around for a car and a place to stay. I'd just as soon keep the peace as long as we need each other."

"Then you've decided to stay? That's great, Shea! Anything I can do to help, just say the word."

"Thanks, Jean." The warm acceptance she'd found with the Cummings family had been a very real factor in her decision. With no family to speak of, friends were important to her.

"You'll need a job. Has Dave said anything about hiring you as a secretary? He's always griping about how much time he spends retyping everything."

"Forget it," Shea said flatly.

"But don't you see—"

Shea recognized the expression immediately. It was the same one Jean had worn when she'd been describing the redheaded widow she'd picked out for her brother. "Oh, no. No way! Jean, it just wouldn't work. In the first place, I'm not looking for a secretarial job. In the second place, even if I were, I could never work for your brother."

"You're already working for him," Jean pointed out with irrefutable logic.

Shea rinsed the potato salad bowl and slid it into the dishwasher. "That's different. He's not paying me anything."

"He's not paying you? Then why on earth are you carting him all over creation, if not for money? Is there something you're not telling me?"

"Hardly," Shea scoffed. "We're simply using each other. He needs a driver—I need transportation. It's that's simple."

The two women finished clearing away, and Shea made her excuses to leave. Jean, unusually thoughtful, nodded absently, and Shea let herself out, waving to a neighbor who was raking the lawn next door. The pleasant scent of burning leaves trailed after her as she drove off in the direction of Folly's End for another look at one of the three empty cottages that stood alone on the barren stretch of beach.

An unseasonable south wind, holding out a tantalizing promise of summer, molded her pink pullover to her body as she got out. Shea lifted her arms, glorying in the warmth, the tangy salt air and the feeling of well-being that lifted her spirits immeasurably. By the time summer arrived, she planned to be settled into her own home, with her workshop all set up and at least one retail outlet for her wares.

The cottage she'd chosen for herself sat slightly apart from the other two. Seen objectively, it might be considered ugly, but Shea had passed the stage of objectivity. After the flamboyant colors of Mexico, the faded green siding struck her as almost sedate. And while there was nothing particularly striking about the boxy shape, the tiny bay window was a decided plus.

If she'd needed a clincher, it had been the price. While it was more than she'd budgeted for housing, the fact that she loved the location and that there were no close neighbors to complain had tipped the scales in its favor. Silverworking could be noisy, and when she was oxidizing, the rank smell of liver of sulfur permeated everything.

Besides, the cost of the motel, while reasonable enough for a night or two, was eating into her meager funds at an alarming pace. The sooner she got settled into her own place and started producing, the better.

Dave waited impatiently for his ride to arrive. If there was one thing clearly designed to drive a sane man wild, it was being at the mercy of a woman driver. She was five minutes late already. At this rate, the tide would be on its way in again before they ever got there!

What the devil had he ever done to deserve this fate? One disaster after another, with no relief in sight. Lady was being stubborn—she refused to walk unless he went with her—and this morning he'd tripped on a root and fallen flat on his face.

In fact nothing had gone right since the hurricane last fall, when he'd slipped on the tower, struck a tree limb and broken his right leg in two places before he even hit the ground.

The trip to New York was another prime example. His publishers had obviously hired a tribe of chimps to set the type, and as if that weren't bad enough, half the charts he'd labored over for months were lost. He'd started in on the galleys and given up before he'd finished correcting the first chapter. It was hopeless. The whole damned thing had to be done over, and it wasn't something that could be handled over the phone.

Then he'd come home to find that he'd inherited Shea.

God knows, the last thing he needed was to be named guardian to anyone, but when it was a woman like Shea, a woman who'd managed to get under his skin to the point where he couldn't even concentrate on his work . . .

"Look after her for me," the old man had written. And Dave had honestly done his best. He'd gone after her and apologized. He'd even delivered himself into her hands instead of getting one of Jean's boys to drive him around, as he'd planned. And what had he earned for his trouble? It had taken no more than a day before she'd started getting to him.

Oh, there'd been nothing blatant, nothing he could put his finger on, but he'd known all the same. She was trouble. Hell, he'd known that the first time he ever laid eyes on her, before he even knew who she was. Only he'd thought it was a simple matter of relieving him of a few pounds of silver.

From that point on, things had gone rapidly downhill. His judgment, usually impeccable, had been way off. He'd made a royal ass of himself, and in trying to make up for it, he'd gotten himself thoroughly tangled in her web.

That guileless look of hers . . . and that mouth. Why the hell couldn't she have had an overbite, or buck teeth, anything that would have given him a fighting chance?

Cold showers, at the best of times, were no real treat. Hopping around on one leg in a slippery bathtub while the other one hung outside the shower curtain was downright hazardous.

Invariably, by the time he finished bathing, drained the tub and commenced the awkward operation of getting himself out again, he was in a steaming temper.

"Same place?" Shea asked breathlessly, driving up to the foot of the crooked brick walk only seven minutes past the appointed time.

Dave grunted and heaved himself in beside her, jamming his crutch down between the seat and the outside of the vintage Jeep. He was beginning to wonder if he'd ever be really mobile again. The Porsche would probably dry-rot before he was ever in shape even to back it out of the garage.

"Yeah, same place," he muttered, ignoring the flush of color high in her cheeks that made her eyes dance like twin sapphires. "Any objections?"

"Who, me, sir? No *sir*, sir, not me!" She could feel his disgruntled mood reaching out like a wet umbrella, but she refused to let it drip all over her joy. This very morning on the way to the hall she'd stopped by the realtor's office and signed the lease. By this afternoon—tomorrow, at the latest—she'd have water, power—the works.

They rode in silence. The soft, warm breeze had shifted slightly to the southeast, moving gray clouds across the sky, but it was still balmy. A little moodiness on Dave's part wasn't going to spoil her pleasure.

She pulled up at the barricade that blocked the broken end of pavement, and for several minutes, neither of them moved. The silence was broken only by the tick of the cooling engine, the strident cry of an oyster catcher and the soft, restless sigh of the surf.

"We keep coming back to this same place every day. Is there some special attraction here?" she asked finally.

Why take it out on Shea? It was his problem, not hers. Unclipping his seat belt, Dave turned to regard her with a glimmer of wry amusement. "You mean aside from the pleasure of my company?"

Shea glanced at him, not quite trusting the sudden thaw. There was so much she didn't understand about this man. Just recently she'd been so caught up in her own affairs that she'd all but forgotten that odd surge of awareness she'd felt on first meeting him. The unexpected hint of humor put her on guard. Kilo Alpha in his natural state of surliness was bad enough. Genial, he just might be more than she could handle.

"Have you thought about what you're going to do?" Dave asked.

"I've done more than think about it."

His thick eyebrows lifted inquiringly. Using both hands, he shifted his cast to a more comfortable position and waited for her to go on.

"See that green cottage? The one on the end?" Shea said with barely concealed pride. "As of approximately one hour ago, it's mine. That's why I was late."

His eyes narrowed swiftly into slits of burnished brass. "What do you mean, it's yours?"

Shea's fingers plucked at a loose thread in the straw seat mat. "It's mine," she repeated, unconsciously seeking his approval. "At least for the next six months it's mine. I signed the lease this morning."

"The hell you did!"

All the expectant pleasure left her face. It didn't matter, she told herself firmly. It was none of Dave's business where she lived. Why should she care what he thought?

His hands bit into on her shoulders and he turned her to face him. "Listen to me, Shea. I'm only trying to keep you from making a stupid mistake."

"Thanks for your concern, but I really don't need it." She had her emotions under control almost before her chin quivered, but she didn't dare let him see how deeply she'd been affected by his harsh words. If he ever discovered how uncertain she really was, she'd never be able to hold out against him. He'd be taking over just the way her grandfather had done, deciding what she would study, who her friends would be, what sort of career she should plan for. She'd been twelve years old then. She was twenty-three now. She had to do this her way, or how would she ever learn to trust her judgment?

For what seemed an eternity, Dave continued to bore into her with those laserlike eyes of his, his hands gripping her shoulders until she began to squirm.

Instantly he released her. More shaken than she dared admit, Shea took refuge in anger. "Look, just because you hired me to drive you around doesn't give you any right to meddle in my private affairs."

"I didn't 'hire' you, dammit. I inher—"

"You're darned right you didn't hire me. You couldn't pay me enough to make it worth my while!"

"If it's money you want—"

"I don't want your money, I just want you to leave me alone."

"It'll be a pleasure!" Yanking open the door, Dave swung himself out, jerking at his crutch while he held on to the door. It jammed under the seat and he swore heartily. By the time he'd managed to extract it, one skinned knuckle and several minutes later, Shea was struggling between tears and laughter.

She watched him hobble off, the rubber-tipped stick sinking deeper with every step. Oh, Lord, what was there about the man that affected her this way? Irascible, moody, suspicious, dictatorial—he was all of that and more. And just when he had her hating him, he'd throw her completely off-balance with a smile so sweet her very bones turned to honey. She couldn't think of a single nice thing to say about the wretched man, and yet he could move her in a way no one else had even come close to.

No point in trying to comprehend the incomprehensible. There was obviously some sort of chemistry at work here. Dave was just as obviously immune to it. Thank goodness for small favors. If it were mutual, she really would be in trouble.

Shea climbed down from the worn seat and, with no deliberate decision, turned in the opposite direction from the one Dave had taken. A walk on the beach should put things into proper perspective. After all, she rationalized, she was still a bit raw from the events of the past few months—her grandfather's death, Inez's last tearful visit, all the things that had had to be done before she left Mexico for good.

Contacting her father had been one of the more painful duties. He'd so obviously thought she'd been looking for a place to go. As if she'd ever go where she wasn't wanted again. Her grandfather had taken her in and given her all the love and guidance she could have wished for—sometimes a bit too much guidance. But she'd always been aware of the fact that he'd had no choice. She'd been dropped on his doorstep like an unwanted parcel, and neither of them had had much choice.

Stooping, she picked up a small piece of driftwood and traced the worn curves with a forefinger. Already she could forsee a subtle change in her designs from the traditional filigree work for which the area around Tuxtla was famous. Shells, driftwood, even the wind-sculpted shrubbery that clung to the low barrier dunes would have an effect. This bit of driftwood, for instance, would translate beautifully into silver.

By the time she got back to the Jeep Shea was feeling immensely more confident. It wasn't as though her plans had been hastily thrown together. This had been no impulse on

her part, but a well-thought-out step on the road to security. Why should she feel defensive just because Kilo Alpha
was in a rotten mood this morning?

Even before she saw him returning, she could hear him
quite clearly. Profanity blistered the air as he hobbled
through the sand, a pair of binoculars beating against his
chest with every lurching step and the slit leg of his jeans
flapping in the wind. He looked as thunderous as the clouds
that were piling up on the horizon. In fact, he reminded her
of a one-legged sea gull she'd seen just yesterday, its hand-
icap somehow magnifying its native fierceness.

Shea waited until he reached the steep shelf where the
tides had eaten away the dune before going to meet him.
Torn between laughter and sympathy, she leaned forward to
extend a hand. "Need some help?"

"No point in both of us coming to grief," Dave grumbled. "Turn your back. I'll get up the same way I got
down." When she didn't move quickly enough, he barked
at her. "Turn your back, dammit! This is embarrassing
enough as it is!"

By the time he secured himself in the passenger seat, she'd
already switched on the ignition. Determined not to let him
get to her, she tried again. "What were you doing out there,
bird-watching?" She indicated the binoculars resting in his
lap.

"Watching the bottom of the ocean change shape."

Shea sent him a disparaging glance. So much for her efforts at polite conversation.

"You asked me what I was doing," Dave said with exaggerated patience. "I told you."

"Oh, sure. X-ray eyes." She slowed up for a turning car,
downshifted and shot past. Fortunately at this time of year
there was little traffic on the beach strip.

Dave reached up and gripped the roll bar that had been installed overhead. "Did anyone ever tell you what a sweet disposition you have?" he asked mildly.

"Often." She took deliberate aim at a pothole and hit it squarely.

"They lied."

"They did not. I do have a sweet disposition."

"Yeah, sweet like those cactus flowers that grow all over the beach." His blistering gaze skimmed her profile, and Shea wondered hopelessly if there would ever come a time when she'd be immune to him.

"Ha! Talk about the pot calling the kettle black," she jeered.

"I've got things on my mind," he said shortly.

"You think you're the only one with problems?" Shea exclaimed, lifting her foot as she felt the accelerator hit the floorboards. "Sorry," she said grudgingly. "I've got things on my mind, too."

"Anything you'd care to share?"

"With you?"

"Is that so unthinkable?" Dave asked in an excessively mild voice. "Keep going," he instructed when she came to the turn she normally took.

Shea prayed for patience. "I think the less we have to say to each other, the better off we'll both be, don't you?"

Resting one arm along the back of the seat, Dave stared again at the familiar lines of her profile. He could have drawn it in his sleep. Observing and recording was an in-grained habit with him, and by now he'd memorized every line of her body, every feature on her face. He noticed, for instance, that the tip of her nose was pink, and for some obscure reason, it affected him strongly. It was a nice nose. It was a nice face. Not startlingly beautiful, but with a quiet sort of loveliness that was all the more effective for being understated.

At the moment she was furious with him, and he couldn't much blame her. God knows, he was no angel at the best of times. The frustration of a broken leg had eroded his temper still further, not to mention frustrations of an altogether different sort.

"Now about this cottage you're considering renting," he began in his most reasonable tone. His eyes sparkled with amusement as he watched her reaction—chin up, chest out, three deep breaths.

"Not 'considering.' I've already signed the papers. In fact, I'll probably be moving in this afternoon."

He frowned, amusement quickly lost under a very real concern. "Shea, I'm not trying to spoil things for you, in spite of what you obviously think. The place is impossible. It's right in the path of one of the most unstable inlets on the middle Atlantic." Not to mention, he added silently, in the middle of a possible drug bust.

"It's at least a thousand feet from the inlet and another thousand from the beach."

Tapping his fingers on the dashboard, Dave considered another approach. "There's more room than I'll ever need at the hall just going to waste. Why not—"

"No."

"The beach is completely deserted this time of year."

"One of it's major assets," she retorted.

"Transportation!" He pounced on that one. She could hardly get back and forth on a bicycle once the weather clamped down again. "Do you have any idea how cold and miserable it can get here in January and February?"

"We're practically in the middle of January," she reminded him. "I think I can manage." She pulled up at the dead end just outside the entrance to Fort Caswell, the site of the last naval battles of the Confederacy. "In fact, I'm managing so well I probably won't be able to drive for you much longer. How long before you're out of the cast?"

"Two weeks," Dave grumbled, wondering how he'd lost control of the situation so quickly. "Look, about this cottage of yours, Shea..."

"It's made to order. There's enough furniture to get by on, especially since one of the bedrooms will be a workshop. Jean's promised to take me around to the yard sales so I can pick up whatever else I need."

Yard sales! The thought of her living alone out there at the end of nowhere was bad enough; the idea of her picking over other people's junk was more than he could bear. "Look, there's a bunch of stuff in the attic—if you need anything, you're more than welcome to it."

The lump that suddenly rose in her throat refused to go away, and Shea turned to stare out at the single patch of blue that was fast dwindling under the encroaching clouds.

Madame Blueskies. What were the words from that old song her grandfather used to sing? "Nothing but blue skies from now on." She'd believed it. She'd been so determined that nothing could go wrong if she planned carefully and resisted making any impulsive moves.

And she had. She'd done exactly that. Only how could she have forseen Dave Pendleton?

Over the next few days Shea tried to pretend that nothing had changed between them. She managed to move into her cottage while still driving Dave wherever he needed to go— to the beach, the post office, the doctor's office.

She refused to invite him in on the grounds that she still wasn't settled. He didn't insist, but he did walk around outside, wrenching loose a dangling section of gutter, a Romance — **more passion, more pleasure, more love.**

Escape to where love is the language spoken from the heart. Discover big, powerful, modern stories brought to you by Silhouette's top selling authors. Now as a Regular reader of Silhouette Special Edition you can enjoy 6 superb novels every month from Silhouette Reader Service — delivered direct to your door, post and packing free, with a whole range of special benefits; a free monthly Newsletter, packed with recipes, competitions, exclusive book offers and information on the top Silhouette authors plus extra bargain offers and big cash savings.

And by way of introduction we will send you four specially selected Silhouette Special Edition novels, plus an exclusive Silhouette Tote Bag FREE when you complete and return this card.

FREE TOTE BAG
as your introduction to
Silhouette Special Edition

Dear Jane,

Your special introductory offer of 4 free books is too good to miss. I understand they are mine to keep with the FREE Tote Bag.

Please also reserve a Silhouette Special Edition subscription for me. If I decide to subscribe, I shall receive six new books each month for £7.50 post and packing free. If I decide not to subscribe I shall write and tell you within 10 days. The Free Books and Tote Bag will be mine to keep in either case.

I understand that I may cancel my subscription at any time simply by writing to you. I am over 18 years of age.

Name _____

Address _____

_____ Signature _____

Postcode _____ 🔔 **7S6SEA**

The publisher reserves the right to exercise discretion in granting membership.
Offer expires — December 31st 1986. You may be mailed with other offers as a result of this application.

YOURS FREE!

Here's the stylish shopper for the real Romantic! A smart Tote Bag in white canvas emblazoned with the Silhouette motif in navy and red. Remember, it's yours to keep whether or not you become a subscriber. Valid in UK only. Overseas please send for details.

Please note, readers in South Africa write to: **Independent Book Services P.T.Y. Post Bag X3010, Randburg, 2125 South Africa.**
Silhouette is an imprint of Mills & Boon Ltd.

NO STAMP NEEDED

Jane Nicholls
Silhouette Reader Service
FREEPOST
PO Box 236
Croydon
Surrey
CR9 9EL

scowling at a loose board, whacking a crooked porch rail with his crutch.

"The place is a wreck," he grumbled. "Any building inspector would condemn it in a minute."

"Considering the condition of Pendle Hall, I'm surprised that you have the nerve to mention it."

"At least there's nothing structurally wrong with my house. This place will wash away with the first high tide."

"I'll keep a life belt handy."

"Yeah, you do that. Fill your pockets with all that damned silver you haul around with you and float on over to the mainland." How could he tell her the real reason he was so concerned? It wasn't the tides. Hell, he'd haul her out of there bodily at the first hint of an abnormal tide. "Look, I've got to go to Wilmington tomorrow," he said, instead. "Think you can handle it?"

"That's perfect!" Shea cried. She'd just been waiting for a chance to look for possible outlets for her work.

"Are you checked out in anything faster than a Jeep?"

"You mean the pickup?"

"I mean an '81 Porsche 928S."

Shea backed away, coming to a halt when her legs bumped against the sloping front porch. "No way. An '81 Chevvie, maybe, but I refuse to drive anything I can't spell."

"P-o-r—"

"Forget it." She dropped down onto the sandy boards. "The Jeep's just fine."

"It might be damp," Dave warned her. "They're predicting more rain."

"I have a raincoat."

Dave moved closer, so close he could catch a drift of the clean, soapy scent of her body. "You also have an exasperating habit of getting your own way." He gazed down at the top of her head as she stubbornly refused to look up at him.

"Shea?"

"Well, whose way should I get if not my own?" she reasoned.

Bending over, he took her face between his two hands and tilted it upward. Shaking his head, he sighed, still not releasing her. It was the same maddening face that had been coming between him and his work from the first time he'd seen it scrubbed clean of all that paint. He didn't hold out much hope for improvement in the near future.

"How about my way for a change?" he suggested, drawing her to her feet.

When his lips first touched hers, Shea gasped audibly. Had he felt it, too—the shock of electricity that arced between them? Before she could draw back, his arms closed around her. The crutch struck the porch and landed silently on the ground, and she reached her arms around his waist, straining to prolong the contact as they swayed together.

Her lips parted, inviting his invasion. The sweet, musky taste of him, the feel of his hard, heated body pressing into her trembling softness, broke through the last threads of her resistance as if they were no more than cobwebs.

His firm mouth played skillfully over hers, exploring, beseeching, demanding. Again and again his lips lifted, only to return as though he couldn't get enough of the taste of her.

Finally, when she was all but reeling from the dizzying spell of him, he drew back, capturing her face between his hands.

"Shea," he whispered, his fingers tangling in her hair as he gazed down at her with eyes gone strangely dark. "Shea, I'm sorry—I didn't intend for this to happen."

"But why?" Before the words were even out she wanted to snatch them back. *Don't plead. For God's sake, Shea, don't beg!*

"Let's just say my judgment isn't always what it should be, shall we? I promise you it won't happen again."

He backed away, grabbed on to one of the leaning porch supports and swung down to retrieve his crutch, allowing Shea the time to collect herself.

Why not? she'd meant. Had he honestly misunderstood her question, or was he just giving her a chance to save her pride?

Her chin came up instinctively and she smoothed back her hair with unsteady fingers. "At least we agree on one thing—it won't happen again."

Dave could have kicked himself. "Look, if we're going to Wilmington tomorrow, maybe I'd better get back and make a few calls. I have a friend there who might be in the market for a secretary. I'd be glad to—"

"Forget it," she said dully.

One look was enough to tell Dave that this was not the time to pursue the matter. Her lips were still soft from his kisses, but the look in her eyes...

God, he ought to be hauled out at dawn and shot. So much for promises.

The drive back to the mainland was anticlimactic. Neither of them had much to say, although Shea dimly recognized the fact that Dave was doing his best to put her at ease with talk of the weather and a reminder to wear a raincoat.

She was acutely conscious of his glowering presence beside her as she skirted Southport and headed north to Pendle Hall. Only the knowledge that he felt as awkward as she did kept her from throwing the keys after him and walking back.

Six

Her newly installed phone was ringing stridently as Shea let herself in the house after delivering Dave to his doorstep. In a state resembling shock, she lifted it from the cradle, her eyes still slightly unfocused. Love? She couldn't possibly be in love with David Pendleton. Infatuation...a strong attraction, perhaps, but *love*? It was against all reason, and besides, it didn't fit in with the careful plans she'd made. There was no room for—

"Shea? Can you hear me? Shea!" Jean's voice filtered into the room, and Shea shook herself free of troublesome thoughts and lifted the receiver in time to hear Jean's succinctly voiced opinion of all machinery.

"I'm not sure telephones are considered machinery," Shea said by way of greeting.

"I thought maybe they hadn't hooked you up right. Look, I just heard about a new consignment shop near Shallotte. Interested in checking it out tomorrow?"

"Tomorrow? Jean, I'm tied up tomorrow."

"Still carting Dave around? I'm surprised you haven't bopped him with his crutch and dumped him in Davis Ditch by now. Impossible, isn't he?"

"Oh, I don't know, sometimes he's almost . . . possible." Shea laughed. Leaning against the wall, she propped a foot on a wicker ottoman, one of the few decent pieces of furniture the cottage contained at this point.

The pause that followed was fraught with meaning, and Shea began mentally throwing up barricades against Jean's predilection for meddling. "Actually, I have some business of my own in Wilmington. I've checked the ads and the yellow pages and picked out several possible retail outlets for my jewelry. I thought I'd check them out before I start producing any—" She broke off at the noise that came clearly through the lines.

Jean yelled out a dire threat to whoever had let Sherlock off his leash, and Shea began to laugh. "Joey, get this creature off my back!"

In spite of the unrelenting rain that had soaked through her raincoat and seeped into her new boots, Shea was brimming with excitement when she picked Dave up on the appointed corner a few minutes past five the following day. She forced herself to ignore the thunderous scowl on his rain-wet face. He hadn't been in the best of moods on the trip to Wilmington that morning, his conversation limited to directions, instructions and a terse admonition when she'd almost missed a turn.

She could afford to be magnanimous after her wonderful luck. Besides, she simply had to share the news with someone, or she'd burst!

Wriggling in her seat, she searched for a casual way to let him know that her career was off and running. And with no help from any friends of his, who might or might not be in need of clerical help.

"You seem to have enjoyed yourself today," Dave grumbled, jamming his crutch into its appointed place beside the seat. Rain soaked his hair, plastering it to his broad forehead. A rivulet made its way down one of the shallow lines that grooved his lean cheeks, and Shea watched in fascination to see if it would curl into his mouth or find its way to the shallow cleft in his chin.

Unconsciously she licked her lips. "You know, on anyone else, those lines would be called laugh lines. On you, I'm not so sure." The words were spoken in a teasing manner. She should have known better.

"Oh, you read facial lines, Madame Blueskies? Then read mine." He turned to glare at her. "What do they tell you?"

Grimacing, she ground the gears and pulled into the stream of late-afternoon traffic. "That things didn't go your way today?"

"That's one way of putting it." Dave fastened his seat belt and settled himself morosely for the ride home. He'd been hoping for a reprieve from the Drug Enforcement Agency. Instead he'd had his worse fears confirmed. DEA had got wind of a big drop somewhere between Baldhead and the South Carolina line. That meant three inlets to cover, with Folly's End right in the middle of the action.

Shea, her own excitement wilting rapidly under Dave's oppressive mood, concentrated on getting them safely out of town. She'd never driven in Wilmington before that day. Traffic hadn't been all that bad when they crossed the bridge that morning, but now it seemed that every car in New Hanover County was on the highway.

With every passing minute she grew more miserably conscious of Dave's presence beside her. One glance was enough to tell her he was ready to pounce on her slightest mistake.

Much later it occurred to Shea that it was probably Dave's critical mood and her awareness of it that had saved both their necks. She'd crept along for blocks of bumper-to-bumper traffic, gripping the wheel with both hands, her glance moving from rearview mirror to rain-blurred side mirrors and back to the fan-shaped patch cleared by the windshield wipers. In Mexico one learned to drive defensively.

It was still pouring as they inched their way toward the main intersection. At the first sound of blaring horns, even before the orderly pattern of traffic ahead of them began to go haywire, Shea reacted by whipping the Jeep into the parking lot of a deserted service station on her right, coming to rest between a garbage dumpster and an enormous live-oak tree. Branches slapped the windshield and scraped against the fenders, as out on the street behind them all hell broke loose.

"Good God!" Dave was panting as though he'd run the distance. "Are you all right?"

"Shaking like a leaf, but otherwise okay," Shea whispered, her voice barely audible in the rapid crescendo of screeching brakes, tangled bumpers and crunching fenders.

"Lady, I don't know where you got your reflexes, but they sure as hell come in handy at a time like this."

"If that had turned out to be a false alarm you'd be singing another tune." Weakly Shea brushed her hair from her face and noticed for the first time that she was trembling. "I think I might have scratched your fender."

"Damn the fender, are you all right?" His eyes devoured her, taking in the sudden pallor of her face, the wide, fear-darkened eyes. Reassured, he turned away, making a visible effort to relax. "If I'm going to get involved in this sort of skirmish, I'd prefer to have something a little more solid wrapped around me—like a tank."

"Did you hit anything?"

"My brake foot almost went through the floor, cast and all. Other than that, no rattles, no pain—guess I'm still intact." He twisted to look over his shoulder as the whine of sirens announced the arrival on the scene of several official vehicles. "Driver's license in order? Technically we weren't involved, but to get out of here, we'll probably have to run the gamut."

The gamut, as it turned out, was short and sweet. With some nine cars involved in a chain collision on the rain-slick streets, there was no time to bother with nonessentials. Shea was able, by driving along the sidewalk and dodging obstacles for half a block, to leave the scene behind them.

"Now what? I'm thoroughly lost." She breathed a sigh of relief as the flashing lights receded into the background.

"Take a left at the next corner and then a right, and keep going for about half a dozen blocks."

Dave directed them to a quiet-looking restaurant, and asking no questions, Shea parked as close to the entrance as she could manage. Only when she pried her fingers from the steering wheel did she realize that she was beginning to shake rather badly.

The smell of food wafted out to the warm, softly lit lobby, and it occurred to her that she'd skipped lunch. She slid out of her raincoat and Dave hung it on the rack. "My boots are squishy," she murmured.

"I think you just lost the last of your suntan," Dave observed as a hostess led them to a corner table. "Sure you're all right? You look more like a ghost than a gypsy."

"There goes my fortune-telling career. Lucky for me I've got something else—" She broke off as a waitress flipped open a menu and placed it lovingly in Dave's hands with a sultry recommendation for the swordfish.

Dave studied the menu while the waitress studied him. After a moment, she tossed the other menu on the table in front of Shea and sauntered away, promising to return with a fresh pot of coffee.

"No wonder your reflexes were so sharp," Dave remarked with the first smile she'd seen from him all day. "Madame Blueskies probably read the whole incident in the palm of her hand before we ever left home." He laid his menu aside and leaned back.

"Madame Blueskies wouldn't dream of predicting the future. She reads character using the twin studies of chirogonomy and chiromancy."

"Using the twin what of what?" He turned to the waitress, who had reappeared with the coffee carafe. The waitress took Shea's order and quickly turned her attention to Dave. "Make that hot tea, will you? A pot of it."

With a smile that promised far more than the menu offered, the woman hurried to oblige. It occurred to Shea that most women would hurry to oblige David Pendleton. His hair was plastered to his head, there were scowl lines etched on his brow, the poor waitress had to step over a crutch and a cast just to get near him, and still she couldn't seem to do enough. She hadn't even spared a glance at Shea.

"She looks as if she could eat you with a spoon," Shea muttered, watching the swing of generous hips.

Dave followed her glance, and to Shea's amusement, his color actually deepened. Gruffly he changed the subject. "Jean swears by hot tea at times like this. With that brood of hers, she's been through the mill."

"I don't mind hot tea." Shea hated hot tea.

"With lots of sugar, whether you usually drink it sweet or not. You're so pale your eyes look like—"

"Don't tell me," Shea broke in dryly. "Like burned holes in a blanket."

"I was going to say, 'like bluebells in the snow,' Madame Fortune-teller. So much for your omniscience."

The gentle teasing, the concern that made him reach out to touch her hand every few minutes, was almost her undoing. Shea took refuge in banter. "You obviously don't have much respect for my profession. You geologists," she scoffed. "Unless it's carved in granite, or—"

"Or written in the sands of time?"

"Or recorded on a lot of charts and graphs," she corrected, "you don't believe it. You probably aren't even aware that the art-science of palmistry predates history." She met his eyes and glanced swiftly away again, disconcerted by the intensity of his gaze. She was nervous enough as it was. If he kept on looking at her, she'd fly into a hundred pieces.

"How can anyone know what predates history?" Dave asked calmly, as if he hadn't just shattered the last layer of her brittle composure.

"Aristotle and Pliny talked about it." She spooned sugar into her tea until it threatened to overflow the cup. Gently he removed the sugar bowl from her hand.

"Which means nothing at all except that they were up on the superstitions of their times." He smiled again, and Shea felt the release of something warm and sweet inside her.

"Even superstitions had to start somewhere," she defended breathlessly. "The trouble with you scientists is that you demand positive, recordable proof before you'll believe in anything. How can you record a—a feeling? An intuitive knowledge?"

"I think that depends on the feeling," Dave replied quietly.

They were interrupted by the arrival of dinner, and Shea snatched at the reprieve. This simply had to stop, she told herself sternly. She couldn't let herself be distracted, not when everything was working out so perfectly. "I didn't have a chance to tell you—" she began brightly.

Their attentive waitress had reappeared with a basket of rolls and hush puppies, which necessitated a careful rearrangement of everything on the small table. That done, she topped off their water glasses, then asked solicitously if they needed more hot water for tea.

"We're fine, thanks." Dave nodded dismissal.

Obviously immune to subtle hints, she went on to recite the dessert menu. "There's French vanilla ice cream, pecan pie and fresh, homemade lemon custard with..." Her heavily made up eyes skimmed the muscular contours above the cast that protruded from under the table. "Whipped cream," she finished breathily.

By this time she was practically purring in Dave's ear, and Shea bit her bottom lip to stifle her laughter until the woman was out of hearing. If there was a slight edge of hysteria in the giggle that finally escaped her, she chose to ignore it. After all, she was entitled. Hadn't they both narrowly escaped serious injury?

"You find something humorous in lemon custard?" Dave asked mildly.

"She's obviously smitten, poor woman. Probably the cast and the crutch. Some women will overlook anything if a man plays on their sympathy."

He stiffened. "Is that what you think I've been doing?"

Still trembling on the edge of laughter, Shea met his gaze boldly. "Have you?"

"Hell, no. Why would I do a thing like that?"

Shea sensed a slight shift in the balance of power and took full advantage of it to tease him. "Maybe you just like whipped cream?" she hazarded.

Without waiting for the check, Dave dug out several bills and tossed them onto the table. "Let's get out of here."

It occurred to Shea as she held the cuffs of her sweater and pushed her fists into the damp sleeves of her raincoat that neither of them had eaten more than a few bites. She'd rearranged the shrimp on her plate and toyed with her salad, and Dave had done little better.

Had she really thought the balance of power had shifted between them? By the time they stood under the canopy, staring out into the neon-colored rain, all the spurious confidence had drained away, leaving her more uncertain than ever.

"You'd better run for it," Dave ordered gruffly. "Don't wait for me."

"But you'll get soaked."

"So? Maybe it will stir up your sympathies." He sounded not so much sarcastic as tired.

Shea wrapped her hands around his arm, drawing comfort from the strength of him even though she could feel his sudden tension. "Dave, I was only teasing. I get a little silly when I'm nervous."

The arm relaxed and she heard him sigh. She leaned her head against his shoulder, needing the physical contact.

"Are you nervous, honey? It's all over, so stop worrying."

"That's what you think," she replied with a small brittle laugh. "I still have to get us home, you know."

The thought of getting behind the wheel again turned her knees to rubber. How was she going to manage? It was raining harder than ever, and she didn't even know how to find the bridge from here, much less the highway that would carry them home again.

If she'd been thrown from a horse, she'd have climbed right back up again, wouldn't she, Shea asked herself as they huddled under the skimpy canopy and waited for a

break in the downpour. *Not on your life,* came the immediate response.

Sliding under the wheel a few minutes later, Shea braced
herself and started the engine. So far so good. Now all she
had to worry about was thirty to forty miles of night driving on strange highways in the pouring rain.

Dave touched her thigh, his hand burning swiftly through
the damp layers of raincoat and jeans. "Take a left. No
point in pushing our luck. We'll stay over and head home in
the morning."

When it came to a contest of wills, Dave won, hands
down. Shea was in no shape to argue. Nevertheless she made
the effort.

"I can't spend the night in Wilmington. I don't even have
a toothbrush."

"There are drugstores," Dave countered.

"And besides..." She searched vainly for another excuse, knowing full well that Dave's suggestion made sense
under the circumstances. Part of her inability to think
straight probably had to do with a lack of food, but with
every nerve in her body quivering she hadn't been able to eat
a bite.

"Look, I don't know about you, but I've about had it,"
Dave said impatiently when she stalled at the exit of the
restaurant parking lot. "I've been standing all day, and my
leg's giving me the devil. Slamming it through the floorboards didn't help, either."

"I think we'd better go by an emergency room and let
them check you over. You might have—"

"Forget it. It's nothing a couple of aspirin and a bed
won't take care of."

"Or maybe it's just another sympathy play?"

Driving north on Market Street, Shea told herself that she
owed him an apology. Under the circumstances she

shouldn't have taunted him. It was a wonder he hadn't taken her head off. Instead he'd given her terse directions and then clammed up, not speaking another word until they pulled up in front of an attractive motel on the edge of a quiet residential district.

It was the only reasonable thing to do, she rationalized again some thirty minutes later as she stared at her reflection in the motel bathroom.

She peered closer. "There ought to be a law against allowing fluorescent lights in the same room with a mirror." She looked wretched—suntan all gone, shadows under her eyes. How could an accident they hadn't even been involved in produce shadows? They hadn't stopped at a drugstore, either, for aspirin or toothbrushes. Dave had been in such an obvious fierce mood she hadn't dared remind him.

At the tap on her door she snapped off the bathroom light, having done what she could with the amenities supplied by the establishment. "What is it?" she called cautiously, one hand on the knob, the other on the chain.

Dave's voice came through the door. "Open up, Shea. I'm about to pour milk shake down my leg."

"'Milk shake'!" Her stomach reminded her that she'd skimped on breakfast, skipped lunch altogether and been too tense to do more than taste the expensive dinner she'd ordered. She unlatched the door and reached for one of the three disintegrating paper bags Dave juggled. "You said the magic password. Come in out of the rain."

"Could I tempt you with a monster burger and all the trimmings?"

"I love monster burgers with all the trimmings. Fries, too?" She swept the small pile of tourist literature from the round table and relieved him of the other two bags.

"The small one's from the drugstore. I bribed the night clerk's girlfriend to pick up this stuff for us. Any objections to a yellow toothbrush?"

Shea's laughter came almost too easily after the emotional roller coaster of the past few hours. "I love yellow toothbrushes almost as much as I love monster burgers. You think of everything."

"I try," Dave replied, swinging a chair around so that he could prop his aching foot on the edge of the bed. His eyes took in the damp cling of her pink pullover, the way her dark-brown hair turned under around her slender neck. Her face had that just-scrubbed look, making her appear almost indecently young. "Sometimes trying's not enough."

Biting into the thick, luscious sandwich, Shea eyed him questioningly, but if there was any covert meaning in the words, he didn't choose to elaborate. "You've already bought me one dinner tonight," she said when she could speak again. "Let me reimburse you for my share of this feast."

She reached for her purse and Dave glared at her. "Don't be so damned independent. You're working for me. Naturally I expect to pay your expenses."

It was the wrong thing to say. Carefully Shea laid down the hamburger, her fickle appetite gone again. "I think I've had enough," she said quietly.

"Eat. Maybe it'll improve your disposition."

"My disposition! You're the one with the temper like— like a crocodile with the toothache!"

"You've been listening to my sister."

"You're darned right I have! She warned me about you before I ever met you. I wish to goodness I'd listened to her." Shea could feel the heat rising to her cheeks as she fought down an irrational sense of loss. Couldn't they be together for ten minutes without coming to blows? She was beginning to sound just like her mother.

"I wish to God someone had warned me," Dave said disgustedly.

Warned him of what? Shea wondered, but she wasn't about to ask.

"All right, all right, I apologize," he muttered. "Chalk it up to extenuating circumstances. Now will you please eat your dinner so you'll have enough strength to get us home in the morning?"

Cautiously they both resumed eating. Shea left her French fries untouched, her burger half-eaten, and concentrated on the chocolate milk shake. She needed something to cool her down.

And she'd actually thought she was in love with this oaf? No woman in her right mind would fall in love with David Pendleton! Especially, she reminded herself, a woman who'd learned early in life what a hell two people could make for themselves when they were completely incompatible.

"How did your interview go?" Dave asked, as though completely unaware of the tension that was pulling her apart.

"What interview?" Shea asked warily.

"Didn't you say you were seeing someone about a job?" Lifting his thigh with both hands, he shifted the heavy cast to a more comfortable position, and Shea, noticing for the first time the grayness that underlay his perennial tan, hoped he'd had the foresight to order some aspirin, too.

"About my work," she corrected. "I suppose you could call it a job, and it went even better than I'd hoped. I was going to tell you."

"So tell me now," Dave invited. He watched her face light up like a thousand watts. He was beginning to see why Ed had been concerned about her. For all her stubbornness and that prickly, hardheaded pride of hers, there was something so damned vulnerable about her. Any guy could come along and spin her a line and she'd probably fall for it, hook, line and sinker.

And God, he'd kill the first one who tried it!

"After two complete washouts I'd almost given up, when I found this wonderful man." Shea leaned across the bed to retrieve her purse, thus missing the look of alarm that crossed Dave's rugged features. "His name is Mr. Leiberman and he owns a boutique called The Craft Cache."

She extracted the roll of flannel in which she carried her samples, and sitting cross-legged on the bed beside his cast, she spread it across her lap. "He really liked this one." She held up a necklace composed of small silver butterflies, the largest of which was inlaid with fragments of abalone shell. "And this." She pointed out an articulated fish pendant suspended from a handmade silver chain. "And he loved this ring. It was my first attempt at lost-wax casting."

Was it deliberate, the way she reached behind her to lay each piece aside, throwing her small, perfectly shaped breasts into prominence? Didn't she know what she was doing to him? Dammit, he was only human, and under the circumstances...

"Watch over her for me," Ed had asked, and Dave had resigned himself to protecting her until he was confident she was able to look after herself. The trouble was, who was going to protect her from him?

Glancing down at the cast on his leg, he answered his own question. Even if he could get out of his obligation to Bellwood, he was in no shape to go after what he so badly wanted. What a hell of a mess!

"Well? What do you think?" Shea waited expectantly for a comment on her work. If she'd had any lingering doubts about her talent—and face it, she had—Hal Leiberman had put an end to them. He'd been generous with his praise, and then he'd gone on to spell out the difference between wholesaling and consignment, offering her a choice.

"You'll get a smaller percentage if you agree to whole-sale, but you'll get it up front on every piece you turn out," he explained. "If you'd rather consign, you'll get a larger cut—eventually—but you don't get a cent until the piece sells."

Needing the cash up front, she'd chosen outright pur-chase, promising to deliver as soon as she started produc-ing once more. Now, still gloating over her triumph, she said, "Well? Should I forget all this and find a job in an of-fice?"

Dave burrowed his chin in his fist. What could he say? For all he knew, this Leiberman was playing her for a sucker. He wished to hell she'd held off until he could check with his friends. When he'd mentioned the possibility of finding her an office job, she'd reacted the same way she had to his offer of a room at Pendle Hall. Of course, she'd been right to turn him down there, and he'd been out of his head to offer.

"It's still not too late," he said. "At least with secretar-ial work, you've got a guaranteed paycheck coming in. Benefits, health plans—a chance to meet people." Some of the bright expectancy went from her face, and he could have kicked himself. "Shea, you don't need me to tell you your stuff is good." The devil with security. Hadn't he felt the same way at her age, desperately needing a chance to prove himself? "Look, what do I know about silver? I couldn't even tell the difference between your family heirlooms and mine."

"Yours were the black ones," she reminded him as she began to repack the jewelry in its protective case.

Dave shifted impatiently, and his cast bumped against her hip. They both apologized at once, hesitated and tried again, only to halt as two pairs of eyes met and clung.

Shea swallowed hard. "You first," she whispered, no longer able to escape his golden gaze.

"I hurt you. I'm sorry," he said, and she knew he wasn't referring to the bump.

Suddenly, without knowing quite how it came about, Shea was on her knees before his chair. "You didn't hurt me," she reassured. *Not yet,* a voice inside her added.

He reached down for her, drawing her up into his arms. "God, Shea, what am I going to do about you?"

Any rational answer she might have made was forgotten in the blazing glory of his kiss. The very air seemed to shimmer, wrapping them in an airless cocoon. Shea, drawn into the fork of those strong thighs, felt the quick rise of his sexual tension as his lips grew ravenous. Sprawled in the chair, with one leg still propped on the bed, he dragged her slowly up his body until she was clinging to him helplessly, taking each thrust of his tongue and wanting still more.

"Oh, God, this is impossible," Dave groaned, tearing his mouth away only to bury it on her throat. His hands stroked feverish patterns over her back, cupping her hips to lift her and hold her tightly against him. "Shea, I've wanted you from the first moment I saw you, but I promised—"

"Hush," she whispered. "Don't talk." As his hands slipped under the bottom of her sweater and moved in slow, incendiary circles up to her breasts, she tugged to loosen his shirttail. She didn't want to talk. She didn't want to *think*. She didn't want to be reminded of all the reasons for not letting herself get involved with a man like Dave.

"I've got to tell you about—" he began huskily.

"No." Feeling her way through the forest of crisp curls on his chest, her fingertips encountered a hardened pinpoint.

As she toyed with the small male nipple, a shudder raced through Dave's body.

"How very much I want to make love to you," he finished when he could speak again.

"Oh, yes, please," she uttered quickly, slamming the door on caution.

"You'll have to help me." He was half lying in the chair, his chest moving visibly with every thundering beat of his heart.

"Tell me what to do," Shea said simply, and he closed his eyes as if in pain.

"Make me stop before we do something we'll both regret," he said through clenched teeth. "God, Shea, help me stop while I still can, won't you?"

Slowly her hands withdrew from his warm, damp flesh. There was no way she could not know of his burning need, resting as she was in the fork of his thighs. Yet he was pushing her away.

Reluctantly she drew back, unable to meet his eyes. It was for the best, she told herself, but dear Lord, how could anything that felt so wonderfully right be wrong?

It's for the best, she kept repeating silently as Dave levered himself awkwardly from the chair and retrieved his crutch.

Turning, he studied her for one long, endless moment, his eyes unreadable in the shadow of his fierce brows. Then, bidding her a clipped good-night, he let himself out into the blowing rain.

For a long time after the door closed behind him, Shea crouched where he'd left her. She stared unseeingly at the ruins of another unfinished meal. If she didn't soon get away from this man, she told herself in a bitter attempt at humor, she'd starve to death.

All in all, she wasn't looking forward to the drive home. Still, she could hardly desert him now, no matter how much she'd like to run and hide.

Seven

The morning came all too soon, and Shea was awakened by a phone call.

"Look, I don't know about you, but my stomach's running on empty," Dave greeted her. "I've ordered a large pot of coffee, ham and eggs, bacon and eggs, grits, biscuits—the works."

"Oh, but I—"

"Weren't you the one who was telling me how important breakfast is not too long ago?"

"I'm not even awake yet," she protested. "My eyes won't focus properly."

"So I'll share breakfast with a cockeyed fortune-teller. Thirty minutes, all right? Oh, and I ordered the whole thing delivered to your room."

"You're too thoughtful," she muttered sarcastically, slamming the phone into its cradle. So she was going to play hostess again, ready or not.

She was decidedly not. Nevertheless, by the time Dave arrived at her door, along with the breakfast order, she was showered and dressed in yesterday's jeans, boots and pink turtleneck. After the first whiff of coffee, she even managed a creditable smile of greeting.

Dave hadn't missed the look she'd given him when she'd opened the door. In spite of her breeziness, she was still wary. Not that he blamed her after the way he'd behaved lately.

When had it started, this constant low-voltage awareness between them? Had it been there right from the start, before he'd even known who she was? Last night it had nearly reached explosive levels. He'd wanted her badly. And after a sleepless night in these less than romantic circumstances he wanted her still.

Dave watched as she stripped the lid from a jelly cup and sampled it from the tip of her knife. What was there about Shea Bellwood that got under his skin? He'd never lacked for women—desirable women, too. In spite of what Jean seemed to think, he was more than capable of finding himself a woman whenever the need arose.

Only this one was different. Young, probably inexperienced, a bit unsure of herself and trying hard not to let it show. And against all reason, this was the one he wanted more than anything he'd ever wanted in his life.

God knows, she deserved better. Even without his obligation to Ed, he'd have hesitated before using the advantage of his age and experience. At thirty-one, he'd come a long way from the mixed-up kid who'd gone racing off for South America and damned near ended up in a Mexican prison...or worse. But even now he was no bargain.

He'd been about Biff's age then, saddled with a load of guilt because he'd fought with his father just a week before his death, and later, saddled with a white elephant of an estate that he couldn't bring himself to unload.

He had Ed to thank for the fact that he'd been given a second chance, and he'd done his best to make the most of it. He'd gone back to school and ended up with a graduate degree in geology. Since then, he'd followed up his thesis on coastal erosion patterns with further studies and gone on to publish two books on the subject, with another one in the works.

For the sake of a caring stranger almost thirteen years ago who'd had the presence of mind to search his pockets before calling the medics—as well as for the sake of Jean's young hellions—he'd agreed to help the DEA keep an eye on any unusual traffic along the low, coastal marshes, using the cover of his work.

"Bacon or country ham?" Shea asked, casting a covetous glance at the latter.

"Bacon, if it's all the same to you." Dave settled himself into the same chair he'd sat in last night and did his best to concentrate on the food before him.

It was a losing battle.

Where was that cool, analytical mind he'd prided himself on? Little Madame Blueskies had pegged him right when she'd said he had an innate distrust of the emotions and a strong urge to be free. He was aware of two powerful urges right now, and neither of them had a damned thing to do with freedom.

"Ready to ride?" he asked when they'd demolished everything on both plates and finished the last of the coffee.

"The sooner the better. Poor Lady's had a long wait."

"I called Jean right after we checked in and had her send one of the boys out to see about her."

For reasons she couldn't begin to fathom, Shea felt her eyes begin to sting. Why was it that any sign of softness from this man affected her like a head cold?

"You'll have to come inside and say hello to her when we get home. She's been missing you."

They met outside a few minutes later. Shea had tucked her new yellow toothbrush into her purse, feeling like an idiot because she knew she'd never part with it. A toothbrush! Of all the silly, sentimental keepsakes.

By the time she turned off at the faded brick entrance of Pendle Hall, the last vestige of self-consciousness had long since fled. Dave was excellent company when he made the effort. He'd told her about his work as a coastal geologist, about the problems confronting developers of oceanfront property and about the migratory nature of the inlets that cut through the narrow barrier islands at frequent intervals.

"I'll show you a chart that will explain why I objected to your leasing a place at Folly's End," he offered as they pulled up in front of the house.

"Are we going to fight about this again?"

Dave laughed. "Honey, I've already conceded that round. I just thought you might be interested in an overview of what's taken place along that stretch over the past twenty years."

Shea was interested in anything he wanted to show her. If she had a brain in her head, she'd drop him off and use the time to shop for the few things she still needed to complete her workshop. Now that she had an order waiting to be filled, she had no time to waste on nonessentials.

Pocketing the keys, she followed him inside, dropping to her knees to embrace the twisting bundle of warm brown fur that greeted them at the door.

"Watch out for that tongue. She'll lick you down to the bone," Dave warned. "I'll go fix her some cereal and milk. Take off your coat and make yourself at home."

Shea got to her feet and brushed the dog hairs from her hands. She'd forgotten just how inviting the elegantly shabby old room was under the clutter of books and newspapers and a few items of masculine apparel.

"Office is through there—what used to be the dining room," Dave informed her, snatching up a shirt and one wool sock as he headed for the kitchen. "Be back in a minute."

Lady followed him eagerly. Left alone, Shea glanced around the familiar room. She hadn't been inside the house since the night he'd accused her of stealing his family silver. Looking back on their less-than-auspicious beginning, she could smile. They'd both been furious at the time. And then when he'd finally realized the injustice of his accusations, he'd been so embarrassed. Funny, the way they'd struck sparks off each other from the very beginning.

If she wasn't careful, Shea reminded herself, stroking a leather wing chair in passing, one of these days a spark would catch fire and she'd go up in flames. Her future was shaky enough without that complication.

"This is what we call an overwash fan," Dave said a few minutes later. "You can see the fanlike pattern all along here where sea tide washed over to deposit new sand." He pointed to a scalloped area of stunted vegetation in the aerial photograph he was showing her. Dozens of similar photographs covered one whole wall of the room.

"Overwash—is that a bad thing or a good thing?" Shea asked, searching for the distinctive pattern of her patchwork roof. It had been shingled with at least four different colors and patterns when various parts had needed attention at different times.

"Depends on your point of view. A good overwash can undermine a house built too close to the surf. On the other hand, it can contribute to the survival of an island by bringing up sand from the continental shelf and depositing it on the sound side. Sort of a gradual westward migration. If there's a barrier that prevents overwash—artificial dunes, sea walls, that sort of thing—you usually get erosion over on the sound side."

"Some of the pale loops go all the way across the highway."

"Did you expect the highway to act as a dam? What do you think happened to the pavement at Folly's End?"

"They ran out of asphalt?" Shea suggested hopefully.

Dave laughed and reached out to brush away a tendril of hair that had fallen forward when she'd leaned over the pictures. "You're whistling in the dark, honey," he teased. His smile slowly faded as his fingers stroked the velvety softness of her cheek.

Abruptly Shea turned to peer out the tall, uncurtained window. "Don't tell me it's going to rain again! You know, it's not the fans and the overwashes that worry me. It's this everlasting rain. My roof isn't put together quite as neatly as it could be."

"Madame Blueskies should have known better than to jump into—"

"Yes, well..." She left herself open for that one, Shea conceded ruefully. "Right now, Madame Blueskies had better try getting herself home before the bottom drops out of those gray skies." Good Lord, at this rate, she'd plow into a tree before she made it to the end of the driveway. Look at her. One touch and she was shaking like a leaf.

Mumbling something about stopping by the grocers on her way out to the beach, she reached for her purse and her hand struck a stack of papers. As they began to slide, she grabbed for them, knocking over a lamp. In righting it, she tipped over a container of pencils that hit the floor and scattered its contents like so many jackstraws.

"Oh, help," she wailed, kneeling to snatch up handfuls of pencils and papers. She clutched them to her breast. "It's got to be the weather. My reflexes have mildewed."

"And you insisted that you weren't a housebreaker," Dave accused, his eyes dancing with laughter. "Hey, watch out—don't stick a pencil through that chart." He lunged forward, planting his crutch on one of the pages that had fallen to the floor. As the paper began to slide on the thin old Chinese rug, he caught himself on the edge of the table, tilting it just enough to deliver the rest of its load to the floor:

At the look on his face, Shea's lips began to quiver. Valiantly she pinched them into a prim line, but it was no good. She began to laugh. The harder she laughed, the more Dave swore, and the more he swore, the harder she laughed, until her eyes were streaming with tears. Still kneeling, she bent over, inadvertently creasing dozens of pages of notes, diagrams and flawlessly typed manuscript.

Sobering at last, she began sweeping up papers and pencils. She clutched them in one hand and blotted her cheeks on her sleeve. Then, drawing in a deep, steadying breath, she blurted out an apology for her share of the damage. "Sorry. Just be glad your typewriter wasn't on the table, too. I'll hand the stuff up to you and you can sort it out, okay?"

"I should have known better than to let any woman into this room," Dave muttered. "It's strictly off-limits, even to housekeepers. Especially to housekeepers," he added.

Lady, who'd come out from the kitchen to investigate, planted herself on a beautifully executed chart of Corncake inlet and the shoals in the mouth of the Cape Fear River.

She gazed first at Shea, then at Dave, her rheumy eyes begging to be let in on the fun.

"I thought you didn't trust housekeepers," Shea said, shoving against the shelty's broad rump.

"A man's got to trust someone," Dave allowed grudgingly.

"Bully for you."

"Sorry. I didn't mean to imply—"

"That I wasn't to be trusted? Look, you did your share of this mess." Shea's voice still registered an unfortunate tendency to wobble. She studiously avoiding looking up from the floor. "Move over, scamp. No, not you," she said when Dave quickly stepped aside.

Gently she slid the chart from under Lady's bushy tail, doing her best to ignore the sock-covered cast and the single well-worn moccasin only inches from her side. Size eleven, at least, she surmised. Large feet, large hands, large temper.

There were several punctures in the crisp surface of the chart, made by Lady's toenails. Leaning over, Shea supported herself on her elbows and began carefully pressing them out with the back of a fingernail. Hours of work—maybe days of work—ruined by a moment's carelessness. It was really no laughing matter.

"Technically speaking," she stated without looking up from her task, "you're the one who dumped this particular chart on the floor. And Lady did the rest. I hope you appreciate all the trouble I'm going to to get the holes smoothed out."

"'Holes'! What holes?" Bracing a hand on her upturned bottom, Dave leaned over her shoulder. "Dammit, I didn't even get a chance to run copies yet."

"It's not too bad, actually. A little tape on the back, a little Liquid Paper on the front, you'll never know the difference. Stop breathing down my neck, will you?"

Dave stood up again, muttering under his breath. After a careful examination of the clutch of papers he still held, he pronounced the damage to them as negligible. His gaze drifted back to the slight figure kneeling half under the table. He found the view of a rounded denim posterior propped on the soles of two small booted feet far too distracting for his own comfort. "That's enough, Shea. I'll rake out the rest later on."

"No problem. After all, I started this avalanche." She reached halfway under the table for an envelope to add to the stack beside her, then hesitated. "Isn't this—" She could never have mistaken that envelope, not after carrying it almost two thousand miles. "You know, Dave, you never did tell me what was in my—"

"Here, I'll take that," Dave muttered, relieving her of the rumpled envelope. "I don't know how the devil it got mixed up with this stuff." He slipped the letter into his pocket.

Resigned, Shea got to her feet, tugging down the sweater that had ridden up during all her efforts. "You're not going to satisfy my curiosity, are you?" She stood before him, hands on her hips, and dared him to meet her eyes.

Looking remarkably ill at ease, Dave brushed a roll of lint and dog hair from one of the pencils she'd retrieved earlier. "I tried a new housecleaning service last week—bonded crew, all male, in and out in three hours flat. Anything I didn't want them messing with, I threw in here, where I could lock it up."

"And that included Granddad's letter," Shea stated, increasingly puzzled by his evasiveness.

"Well, sure," he said, and to Shea's amazement, a flush of ruddy color suffused his tanned features. "My personal mail—I mean, Ed was a good friend, and—"

"And he was my grandfather. But he didn't write me any letters."

"Why should he? He saw you every day."

"He talked to you once a week on the radio. If he had anything to say, why didn't he tell you himself instead of sending me off on a wild-goose chase?" It was a question she'd asked herself a hundred times. So far she'd come up with no real answer.

"There are some matters that aren't open to public discussion," Dave reminded her, and Shea wasn't sure if he meant it as a rebuff or an explanation. The color was beginning to fade from his face, but he seemed to be having trouble meeting her eyes.

All of which made her more curious than ever...not that she had any right to ask. If Dave had wanted her to know what was in the letter, he'd have told her. It was really none of her business. All the same, since she'd gone to so much trouble to deliver the thing, the least he could have done was offer to share it with her.

"Look, Shea, I've got some work to do here that's going to keep me pretty well tied up tomorrow. The Jeep's all yours."

Her disappointment over the letter gave way to disappointment of another sort. She covered it with a wide-eyed smile. "Wonderful! If you're sure you won't need me, I'll get on with all the shopping I've been putting off."

"You do that," Dave said briskly. "Call Jean. She'll be glad to show you the best places to find whatever you need."

"Good idea," she agreed, trying for the same tone. "I've been meaning to ask her where I could get myself a new propane torch and a good used car."

Shea took great satisfaction in watching that clefted, aggressive jaw drop as she collected her purse and left the room.

"Hey, wait a minute, what was that about a propane torch? What used car?" Dave hobbled after her, catching her just as she let herself out the front door. "Shea, come back here!" he roared, waving his crutch.

"Give me a call when you need me to pick you up," she called out gaily. The smile she sent him as she swung up into the Jeep was a work of art. It was still in place when she roared off down the drive. Halfway out to the highway, it drooped and disappeared.

Actually, she consoled herself as she followed the familiar route, she really did need to finish setting up her workshop now that she had an order to fill. Her old shop equipment hadn't been worth what it would have cost to ship it, but she'd already ordered a new buffing and polishing unit, a supply of the rouges and tripoli needed for finishing her work, as well as several specialized tools she'd been unable to bring with her. The rest could probably be found in any good hardware store.

As for the other item on her shopping list, the time was fast arriving when Dave would no longer need someone to drive him around. By that time she'd need to have made other arrangements. A bicycle might get her around the immediate neighborhood, but it would hardly do to deliver her work to Wilmington.

Her phone began to ring before Shea had even closed the door behind her. It would be Dave, of course, wanting to pick up the gauntlet where she'd flung it when she'd walked out.

She'd behaved childishly. There was no denying that fact. On the other hand, Dave had sounded just like her grandfather, treating her as though she weren't capable of crossing the street without having her hand held.

Overprotectiveness from her grandfather had been understandable, if not particularly enjoyable. He'd been part of a generation that believed in cosseting their women. Add to that the fact that he'd spent the last thirty-five years of his life in a country where docile women and domineering men were the accepted norm, it was no wonder he'd thought he had to make every single decision for her.

But enough was enough. Shea had her own ideas about her immediate future, and they didn't include male nursemaids—no matter how attractive they were. It was enough that she was dangerously infatuated with the man, without delivering herself into his hands like a lump of putty.

She considered picking up the receiver and letting it drop again, a rude but possibly effective way of getting her message across. Instead she clenched her fists and did her best to ignore it. Surely he'd give up eventually.

On the twelfth ring she gave in. Snatching up the receiver, she didn't give him a chance to start in on her again. "Dave, I don't want to talk about it! You seem to think I need a keeper, but..."

A certain quality in the ensuing silence gradually worked its way through her defensiveness. She began to twist the cord between her fingers. "Dave?" she said tentatively. "Did you hear what I said?"

"Hmm," Jean said thoughtfully. "And how *was* your night in Wilmington?"

Oh, Lord, why couldn't she learn to take aim before she fired the first round? "Hello, Jean. Wilmington was wet. How'd you know I was there?"

"Dave called last night about Lady. He didn't ask one of the boys to drive him, and I didn't think he'd suddenly sprouted wings. Getting under your skin, is he? Can't say I didn't warn you."

Shea had to laugh at that. "Actually, it was his disposition you warned me about. You forgot to mention the Caesar complex."

"Oh, so that's how things are."

"Jean, I don't know what you're trying to imply, but..." Shea braced the heel of one boot against toe of the other one and managed to wriggle a foot free. After a thorough soaking, her brand new boots were probably ruined for good.

"Would I stoop to implication?" The injured innocence was a bit overdone.

"On second thought, that's not your style, is it? Knowing you, you'd come right out with whatever was on your mind." Shea had quickly learned that subtlety was hardly one of her friend's most notable characteristics.

"As for what's on my mind," the older woman went on, "I've blackmailed Pete into taking me out to dinner next Friday night to celebrate my birthday. And before you ask which one—don't. I want you and Dave to make up the rest of the party."

"Oh, Jean..."

"Just hold your horses now. If it's Dave you're worried about, relax. I've been managing my baby brother since the day he was born, and I haven't forgotten how to crack the whip."

"In case you haven't looked just lately," Shea retorted dryly, "your baby brother's all grown up." Was he ever!

"Which is why my method works so well," Jean informed her smugly. "The first time he steps out of line, I'll start in on his baby stories, and I guarantee you, he'll back down, meek as a lamb. I've got enough on that man to ensure his good behavior for the next two hundred and fifty years."

"I take it he was a bit wild?" Shea said with a delighted chuckle.

"Wild enough to keep my boys in line. There's nothing they can come up with that he didn't think of first—and probably try. And don't think they don't know it. With Pete on the road sometimes for weeks at a time, Dave's been a lifesaver. They'd never admit it, especially after he's come down hard on them for some harebrained stunt, but all five of those boys think Dave's the absolute tops."

Shea considered the revelation. It might explain his attitude to some degree. At twenty-three, Shea was only four years older than Biff. But those four years made a world of difference—the difference between being a child and being an adult.

"When did you say this birthday party of yours was?" she asked finally.

Jean told her, mentioning the name of one of the area's best restaurants. "No gift, though. Promise?"

"I'm not promising a thing, so don't crack your whip at me." She'd do something special, something in sterling that would look nice on the lapel of Jean's best tweed suit.

"Goodie. I thought I ought to give you an out, but I love gifts. The boys will give me a new electric can opener and Pete will tell me to get what I want. Oh, and by the way," Jean added as Shea began a one-handed wrestling match with her remaining boot. "I'm hot on the trail of a watchdog for you. Any preferences?"

The boot came off suddenly and flew across the room. "What do you mean, a 'watchdog'?"

"You know . . . yap-yap, snap-snap? Dave said—"

"*Dave* said! I might have known. Look, Jean, I appreciate the offer, but a watchdog is the least of my worries right now. I've got the rest of today and all of tomorrow free, and I need to get on the ball. Do you happen to know of a reliable used-car dealer?''

Several hours later, Shea drove herself home, the proud owner of an eleven-year-old four-door sedan with little to recommend it other than the fact that it ran like a dream. According to the mechanic, a ponytailed young man named Tinky, it was a steal. He'd been saving it for his mother, he said, but she'd bought herself a Lincoln demo, instead, just because she liked the color better.

"The touch of rust adds character," Shea told herself, admiring her freshly waxed pea-green car. Her gaze moved on past the massive hood to the pair of yellowing palms she'd just planted. She'd bought them on sale to brighten up her front yard. A few more shrubs, perhaps a flowering vine or two, and no one would even notice the missing shingles and the patchwork roof.

All in all, she told herself proudly, it had been a successful day's shopping. Jean had picked her up right after lunch, and once Shea had managed to satisfy her that absolutely nothing of any significance had taken place the night before, they'd covered ground with admirable efficiency.

A day later, Shea took a break from bending over the workbench that had been delivered early that morning. It had taken her all morning to get it set up properly. She'd tacked the order from Hal Leiberman, with its impressive Craft Cache letterhead, on the wall just above the bench, and started in on the first pair of earrings.

Rubbing the tired muscles of her back, she stared through the window at the spectacular sunset. She still had trouble believing that she was actually here, in a place she'd never even heard of a month ago, living in a home of her own, doing the kind of work she'd dreamed of doing while she'd studied typing, bookkeeping and shorthand by day, and design, lapidary and silverworking at night.

The winding shallows of Big Davis Canal picked up the sunset's gold and crimson, trailing the colors through the surrounding marshes like a carelessly flung scarf. Shea was still admiring the view from her workshop window, when she heard the sound of a car pulling into her sandy driveway. Most of the traffic that came this far was of the four-wheeled variety. This one had the sound of something with a more impressive pedigree.

She was halfway to the door when she heard the gritty footstep on her porch. Of all times for a caller. She was filthy!

Wiping her silver-blackened hands down the front of her old pink smock, she reached for the door just as it rattled under the force of a determined set of knuckles.

"Shea, are you in there?"

Dave? He must have had someone drop him off, but why? Shea fumbled with the latch and threw open the door. "Did you—"

He was alone. There was a racy-looking sports car parked just behind her own car, which was parked behind the Jeep.

The last blaze of color from the evening sky stained his tanned face a deep copper, highlighting the arrogant arch of his nose, the sun-bleached ends of his thick, unruly hair. Under the bulk of an oiled-wool pullover, his shoulders looked more intimidating than ever.

Shea took refuge in anger. "You should have called," she said irritably. "I would have come for you." Dammit, he could have given her enough warning to change into something decent and wash her face and hands, she fumed, leaning around him to see who was waiting in the car. It appeared to be empty, but with the glare on the windshield, it was hard to see.

"Who's your company?" Dave demanded. Through narrowed eyes, he flashed a searching glance about her small living room.

"I don't know what you're talking about, or even what you're doing here. If you needed me today, why didn't you—"

With all the subtlety of a grizzly bear he lifted her by the waist and set her outside, blocking her entrance with his body when she tried to get in again.

Shea had had enough. "Would you mind telling me what you're doing? You barge in here like gangbusters with that Clint Eastwood look on your face—Dave, I'm warning you, I'm in no mood to play cops and robbers. I've been working all day and my—"

"Who's car is that in your driveway?"

"It's *my* car. Whose did you think it was?"

He turned to her then, holding the door for her to come inside. At any other time Shea might have appreciated the play of uncertainty that flickered in his eyes. But not this time. This time he'd gone too far.

"Yours? Shea, you didn't," Dave said flatly. The aggressiveness seemed to drain from his body even as she watched. "You wouldn't pay out good money for that rusty old gas guzzler."

"I wouldn't?" she repeated, her voice ominously quiet.

As if sensing that he might have gone too far, Dave stepped back, and it was then that Shea realized just what was so different about him. "You're not wearing your crutch—I mean, you've lost your cast."

"I know that. Now about that car, Shea, you should have waited until I could go with you."

"David," she said in a low, warning voice.

"What I meant was—well hell, you ought to know better than to jump into something without even thinking it over first. Ed said you were impulsive, but—"

"Ed said what?" Shea felt as if the ground had suddenly opened up right before her feet. "When did he say that? Why should he say it to you?"

Dave reached for the arm of her wicker chair and carefully lowered himself onto its flowered cushion. Away from the deceptive rays of the sunset he looked paler than usual.

Shea noticed the lines of strain on his face. He wasn't supposed to come out of that cast until early next week, but with his usual arrogance, he'd probably stormed into the doctor's office and issued an ultimatum.

Well, sympathy wouldn't get him out of this spot. "Now what's all this business about my grandfather? When did he talk to you about me?"

Dave ran a finger inside the neck of his sweater, as if it had suddenly grown two sizes too small. "Honey, buying a car isn't exactly the same thing as buying a new pair of shoes."

"Don't you 'honey' me, you—you Kilo Alpha! Answer my question!"

"Well, naturally Ed mentioned you. I don't know if he ever told you, but I spent several months with him about a year or so before you came to live with him. In fact, it was Ed who got me started in radio. After I got my ticket, we used to talk almost every night. I practiced my CW—that's my code work—"

"I know what CW is," Shea interjected impatiently. "Go on with your story." For the first time since she'd met him, she felt as if she were actually getting to the heart of something that had stood between them from the first moment—or at least the second. Or maybe the third.

"Well, as I said, Ed mentioned this granddaughter of his who had come to live with him. Then he went off the air for several months," he added, hoping this would get him off the hook.

"That must have been when we moved to a larger house so that Inez could live with us. Go on, go on."

Dave shrugged. How the devil could he tell her anything without telling her all of it? The truth was, the old man had resented the imposition at first. Springing a child on a man in his sixties, a man who'd lived alone for years . . . Well, it was understandable that he'd just as soon not have been burdened with a fresh set of problems at his time in life.

Not that he'd complained. And to his credit, he'd soon come to care for the homeless child he'd inherited. "He was proud of your achievements in school. He used to boast about how easily you caught on to the language."

Unconsciously Dave began to knead the protesting muscles of his right thigh. He'd been so damned eager to get back in shape so he could do something that he'd jumped the gun. At the rate he was going, he might as well have waited.

"Well? Is that all?" Shea asked, arms crossed under her breasts.

It occurred to Dave that the pink embroidered thing she was wearing was probably a lot more revealing than she suspected. She wasn't making things any easier for him, muscle spasms or not.

"You know how it is . . . with half the world listening in and the other half waiting for you to clear the band so they can hop on the frequency, you don't go into details on personal matters."

Shea sighed and dropped her arms to her sides. "Well, he was right. Sometimes I am too impulsive, but I'm working on it. And before you start in again, the car was not one of my impulses. I've been thinking about it for days.''

Yeah, just the way she'd thought about her choice of a cottage for days, Dave thought, resigned to watching her make one mistake after another. She'd barged ahead without even bothering to ask his advice. But God, he was so relieved to find her alone and all right.... Considering the possibilities that had run through his mind when he'd seen that disreputable-looking piece of junk in her driveway, getting suckered in a car deal or even blowing a bundle on this patchwork chicken crate seemed negligible.

''Okay, no more about your car. How about a guided tour, now that you've finally allowed me inside.''

Now that she'd finally allowed him inside. The words etched themselves on Shea's mind. She'd done it, all right. That was precisely what she'd done. She'd not only allowed him inside her house, but inside her life. And as if that weren't bad enough, she'd blundered into the ultimate mistake of allowing him inside her heart, as well.

Eight

———

The guided tour," Shea said, knowing full well the dangers of allowing him to stay one moment longer. She'd been careless enough to fall in love with the man. There was no help for that. As for what happened from here on out, that was a different matter. At this point she was still in control of the situation. It was the thought of losing that control that both terrified and enticed her.

"There's not a lot to see—you don't even have to move from your chair." The chair itself was one of two that had come with the cottage. Someone had painted it an unlikely shade of lavender and covered the cushion with a splashy jungle print in shades of green.

"The bedroom." She nodded to a door on the left. "Bathroom," she continued, indicating the one just beyond it. "The other room's my workshop, and the kitchen you can see for yourself," she finished, waving a hand in the direction of the L-shaped kitchen-dining space. Grimacing, she tucked her filthy hand behind her back.

Supporting himself on the worn arms of the chair, Dave managed to get to his feet without disgracing himself. He glanced around at the freshly scrubbed walls, the hodge-podge of summery furniture, the driftwood and shells that littered the windowsills. How was it that she could throw together a few broken conch shells, a handful of half-dead plants and someone else's cast-off furnishings and come up with something so livable, when his own twelve-room house, filled with valuable antiques, had all the warmth of a drive-in gas station?

He touched a wilted gaillardia she'd dug up on the beach and replanted in a cheap Mexican pot, the sort that could be found at any variety store. "It won't live, you know."

"So now you're a plantologist?" Shea lifted her head proudly. Every line of her slender body was a challenge to him.

"I know beach vegetation. I know this particular species won't get enough sun in a north window." Driven by a sim-mering excitement he couldn't begin to understand, Dave accepted the challenge that was Shea Bellwood. He eyed her steadily.

Words, Shea thought. They were dueling with words, but on a level that had little to do with plants and houses and north-facing windows. She picked up the pot and crossed to the south-facing bay window, placing the plant carefully on the table between a bowl of red onions and an Audubon field guide. "Any other suggestions? Maybe the chairs should be switched, the yellow one over there and the lav-ender one here by the table?"

"Did you by any chance happen to glance at your real-tor's palm long enough to read his character before signing the lease to this place?"

"I think you'd better leave before I forget that you were once a friend of my grandfather's," Shea said quietly. She could have wept. Of all the men in the world, why did she have to fall in love with an obstinate, contentious, hard-headed— The only time they weren't fighting was when they were embracing or eating each other.

As if he knew he'd overstepped the bounds again, Dave took a deep breath and crossed to the door of her bedroom. "So this is where you sleep, hmm?" His rather forced smile lasted just long enough for one quick look inside. "Shea, I told you there was plenty of furniture for the taking at my house. Why didn't you let me know you needed a bed?"

"I have everything I need," Shea informed him. "Your driver's probably getting tired of waiting outside, so don't you think you should be going?"

Small patches of color appeared in his cheeks. "There's no one waiting for me, Shea. I drove myself out here."

She was horrified. She didn't know much about broken bones, but it was easy to see that he was in no shape to drive. "And you accuse me of being impulsive," she marveled. "You couldn't even wait until your appointment next week to get out of that cast, and then the first thing you do is jump in a car and take off. You've go no more judgment than a horsefly!"

Abashed, Dave took his medicine like a man. He deserved it, and she was obviously enjoying the chance to dole it out. When she calmed down, he relinquished the support of her bedroom doorway and turned to the other room that opened off the living room. "I meant it about the bed, Shea. You don't have to sleep on the floor."

"No, I don't have to sleep on the floor," she snapped at him, exasperated because she couldn't stay angry at him for more than a few minutes, no matter how much he deserved it. "That's a brand new mattress in there, and there's nothing wrong with having it on the floor. Lots of people sleep on the floor—it's good for what ails you."

Why on earth was she standing here arguing with him about her sleeping arrangements? If only he knew, she'd probably sleep on top of a sand dune in the middle of winter if he were willing to share it with her. "If you'd care to see where I work, I'll show you," she announced stiffly, brushing past him to switch on the overhead light. While they'd been fighting, the sun had set, turning the sky to a deep, velvety purple.

"The bench isn't finished yet, but this is where I'll do my grinding and polishing." She indicated the workbench that had been delivered just that morning. "The motor will bolt down here. This is the soldering area." She touched the ceramic pads and pointed to the rest of the equipment. "Later on I plan to get a drill press, but for now I can manage with a vise and a good electric drill."

"Is this place wired for all this?" In spite of himself, Dave was impressed with the orderly, workmanlike setup.

Shea felt his reluctant approval and blossomed under it. She knew what she was doing; she'd been preparing for it long enough. "The only thing that pulls a load is the grinding unit, and it's only a one-third-horsepower motor, but that's all I need. It has its own dust collector, too."

"And this thing?" Giving in to the cramping muscles in his right calf, Dave leaned his back against her workbench and propped his foot up on the stump she'd managed to drag in off the beach. She'd pounded three circular indentations of varying sizes into its surface.

"It's for cupping. I lay a flat silver disk over the proper cup and start hammering." She indicated a neat row of assorted mallets lined up behind him. "The bench was my real find. My friend at the used-car place let me have it for practically nothing. He didn't need it anymore.''

Her "friend at the used-car place." Dave closed his eyes and offered up a silent prayer for patience. "Getting back to your car, Shea, would you mind my asking how much you paid for it?"

"Why?"

"Because it's just barely possible that you might have got stung," he said with all the restraint he could muster.

"I didn't. It's a good car. It's not very pretty and it does smoke a little, but it has a lot of miles left in it, and my friend at the used car place is going to arrange for me to buy secondhand motor oil for practically nothing, which he says will do just as well in an engine this old. And anyway," she added, "it's not as old as your Jeep."

Dave swore under his breath. "That's different."

"Why?" Shea asked calmly.

"Because—well, because it is, dammit!"

"Dave, you're yelling. Stop yelling at me, and stop treating me as if I were a child. I know my house isn't up to Pendle Hall standards, but believe me, people live in far worse places and manage to survive. And my car is a mess, but it's my mess, and Tinky promised me—"

"'Tinky'!" Dave exploded.

"My friend at the used-car place. He's the mechanic there. Tinky promised me he'd keep it running."

"Oh, sure he did. You have him on an annual retainer, I suppose."

"We have an arrangement."

"Oh, for crying out loud," Dave groaned. Hitching the leg of his corduroys up, he began massaging the wasted muscles of his calf. He should have stayed away. He should have stayed clear of everything connected with Shea Bellwood until he could figure out how to deal with whatever it was that had happened to him. One look at her and all he wanted to do was take her in there to that mattress on the floor and make love to her. Was that any way to look after her?

Ed had been out of his mind to send him a twenty-three-year-old woman with a maddening way of getting under a man's skin and ask him to *look after her*.

"What are we fighting about?" he asked tiredly.

"I'm not fighting. You are. Does that hurt?" She nodded to his leg.

"I think I may have strained something. This is my first day of driving, remember?"

"You're looking for sympathy? After a reckless stunt like that? I'm beginning to see what Jean meant when she said she had enough on you to blackmail you for the next two hundred and fifty years." Her smile dripped pleasurable malice.

"Jean's just jealous because she got married right out of school and started procreating. She's regretting all the things she's missed."

"You didn't miss much, according to her."

"Are you asking?" Brushing down his pant leg, he crossed his arms and braced them on his knee, studying her under the merciless glare of a naked two-hundred-watt bulb.

Shea met his quizzical gaze and quickly dropped her eyes, only to have them fall on those capable hands of his. *Careful, careful—don't get in any deeper,* she warned herself. The warning went unheeded. "And if I were?"

"What would you like to know? Names, dates, places?"

Shea felt herself coloring, but before she could come up with a retort, Dave leaned away from the bench and gathered her in his arms.

"Shea, why do we affect each other this way? Would you believe that I'm a pretty easy guy to get along with as a rule?"

"Not in a million years." She had to laugh. Caught against the solid warmth of his broad chest, she gazed up at the proud arch of his nose, the aggressive thrust of his clefted chin, and shook her head. "You must think I'm gullible if you expect me to believe that."

"I think you're . . ." The words trailed off as the darks of his eyes widened. His hands clasped her face, tilting it to his.

At first the kiss was almost tentative, as if seeking to explore the source of this elusive magic that sparked so quickly between them. Reaching up, Shea stroked the resilient muscles of his shoulders. There must be words to describe what was happening to her, but they were beyond her knowledge.

Dave's mouth moved experimentally over hers, pressing, nibbling, his tongue tracing the line between her lips until he gained the entrance he sought. Held closely in his arms, Shea felt the last door to safety close behind her, leaving her trembling on the edge of something so beautiful, something so elemental, that she was helpless to resist. Where he led, she could only follow, trusting him to see her through.

The taste of him was sweet and faintly spicy, wildly intoxicating. Her fingers tangled in his thick, warm hair, tugging his head downward so that she could kiss him more thoroughly.

"Ah, Shea—God, sweetheart, have you cast a spell over me?" Dave nipped at her lower lip and then assuaged the small hurt with his tongue. "I could devour you, and I'd still be hungry. What have you done to me?"

Nestled in the haven of his arms, with the virile contours of his body imprinted on her softness, Shea was only too aware of what she'd done to him...of what he was doing to her. Since the very first touch, the first kiss, he'd been like a fever in her blood, and no matter how much she willed it otherwise, each new exposure to him only made matters worse.

"I—I think it's more a case of what have we done to each other," she whispered, sliding her hands up under his sweater and the knit shirt he wore underneath, to touch the muscles of his chest.

Dave caught his breath as her small, capable hands began to move through the pelt on his chest, flicking back and forth across sensitive nerve endings. As soon as she realized the effect she was having on him, she began to smile, the sweep of her lashes covering those passionate blue eyes of hers. "Or what we'd like to do to each other," he countered, his voice unsteady as fresh tremors raked his powerful frame.

He'd managed to unbutton her smock, and now he slipped it back over her shoulders. Just as he'd thought, she wore nothing under it. She was incredibly lovely, her skin as translucent as moonlight, with the pale pink tips of her small breasts growing taut with desire before his very eyes.

"See how well they fit the palms of my hands?" he murmured huskily. Cradling the slight weight, he paid homage to first one, and then the other, tantalizing them with his thumbs and his lips until they hardened into tiny rosebuds.

Leaning against the workbench, Dave gathered her fiercely to him, pressing her hips against the throbbing heat of his thighs. "I can't get you close enough," he said with a groan.

"I know, I know." Struggling with his heavy wool sweater, Shea managed to get it up around his chest. Dave ripped it over his head, taking with it the shirt he'd worn underneath.

"That's better," Shea said as her hands slid up over the smooth surface of his back, savoring the strength of him.

"You're so small. What if I stood you on that stump?" Dave's hands dropped to her sides, and he lifted her easily, swinging her up onto the sturdy chunk of wood. "Hmm, that's much better." Leaning forward, he buried his face in her breasts, wrapping his arms around her hips.

Shea laughed breathlessly and the sound was all mixed up with whimpers of pleasure as the tip of his tongue began to stroke a sensitive nipple. From there he followed an imperceptible line down to the waist of her jeans, nuzzling, nibbling, driving her wild as he forged his way toward the melting core of her desire.

Suddenly he stiffened, and Shea opened her eyes in time to see a flush of pain cross his angular features. "Sweetheart, I don't think this is going to work out. I'd forgotten about this damned leg of mine."

"Maybe you'd better sit down." Concern overtook other considerations as Shea prepared to jump down, but Dave was already shaking his head.

"I just need to rethink my strategy," he told her. "There's got to be an easier way to do this."

With the spell he'd been weaving on her body partially broken, Shea moved back as far as his arms would allow. They were still linked about her hips, and the top of his head was now resting between her breasts. He was breathing heavily, as though he'd just run a marathon.

Gazing down on the back of that proud head, Shea felt her heart contract with emotions she could barely comprehend. A small tuft of hair, lighter than the rest, lay curled in the hollow of his nape. She touched it, the sensitive pads of her finger leaving the silken ends to follow the oddly vulnerable valley until it was lost in the swelling muscles of his back.

Oh, God, she loved him so much she ached with it, even knowing that he could spell the ruin of everything she'd worked for.

"Maybe we both need to do some rethinking, Dave." If only he weren't so domineering. If only he weren't so magnificent! If only, Shea concluded sadly, she weren't so susceptible to him. "Dave, I think you should know that I'm no more anxious to get involved than you are," she said, wondering how she could make him believe that after the way she'd acted. "Jean called you a loner. Actually, that's something I can understand. You see, I—I'm something of a loner, myself."

Tell me that's not true, she pleaded silently. *Tell me it's safe to love you, safe to let myself believe in you.*

With a heavy sigh, Dave stood up, still not releasing her. Shea found herself unable to meet his skeptical look. She licked her lips nervously, and his arms tightened around her. Before she could resist, he tugged her against him, and once more she felt the waters close over her head.

"What are we going to do about it?" he asked. Swinging her down from the stump, he lowered her along his body until her toes touched the floor. "What the devil am I going to do with you, sweetheart?"

"You make me sound like some sort of neighborhood nuisance—like a barking dog." Her lips were against the warm, damp flesh of his throat, and she touched him quickly with the tip of her tongue, savoring the salty, masculine essence of him.

"It's really funny, isn't it?" Dave said tiredly. He laughed. At least she thought he laughed—the sound seemed torn from the depths of him, compounded of pain, irony and a frustrated libido. "God, if you only knew how funny," he said as his hands moved up from her hips to trace the curve of her waist, coming just under her breasts before beginning the downward trek again. "What I'd really like to do is kidnap you and stash you somewhere all to myself and make love to you until I found out what there is about you that drives me up the wall this way."

"I'm not sure if you're trying to flatter me or frighten me." She could feel the swift, fierce rise of his desire, feel her own helpless response begin all over again. His hands, moving in slow patterns along her sides, curved over her hips and then trailed upward until his fingers just brushed against her breasts. He didn't touch them, didn't cup them or kiss them, and already they ached for the feel of his caresses.

Oh, yes, she was in love with him. Not infatuated. That would have been bad enough, but she could have handled that. Love had a different texture; love was for nurturing, not for clutching with greedy hands before it could slip away.

"Dave," Shea began tentatively. She was torn with uncertainty, knowing that she was probably going to jump off the deep end, whether or not he was there to catch her. "Are you sure this is what you want?"

His arms tightened. She could feel his ribs, his heart pounding against her breast, the bold thrust of his masculinity that told her exactly what he wanted from her.

"You doubt it?" A ragged thread of amusement ran just under the dark surface of his voice. "Sweetheart, my leg may still be weak, but there's nothing wrong with the rest of me. We both know what I want. We both want the same thing." He paused. Leaning back, he questioned her with his eyes, offering her a last chance to back out. "Don't we?"

What choice did she have? They were totally incompatible in all but this one area. Besides, this was all he was offering her.

Dave leaned back against the workbench, wincing as his naked back came in contact with the cold steel of a small bench vise. "If it's all the same to you, I think we'd better adjourn to someplace a little more suitable for what I have in mind."

"Are you going to make love to me?"

"Did you ever doubt it?" Dave pressed the tip of a finger to her swollen lips, stroked it over the rounded contour of her chin, down the brave line of her throat, and then trailed it slowly between her breasts, stopping only when he reached the waistband of her jeans.

"I guess it was inevitable, wasn't it?" Shea sighed. She'd already lost control of the situation. Whether they did or didn't, she was no longer in control of her own life. She might as well make the most of it.

As if sensing her uncertainty, Dave tilted her face to meet his. With a tenderness that shattered the last of her doubts, his mouth settled over her parted lips.

Shea swayed in his arms, driven by a desire beyond anything she'd ever dreamed. Tentatively she touched his front teeth with the tip of her tongue, and as if that were the signal he'd been waiting for, Dave deepened the kiss until she felt her very consciousness begin to waver.

Hungrily she drank from his lips, exploring the tastes and textures of him as avidly as he explored her. Each thrust of his tongue brought with it a deeper hunger, a desire to know more, to release more, to discover everything about him.

"We're going to make love to each other," he corrected her after endless moments. "For days now, all I've been able to think of is what it would be like to lay you down and make love to you until nothing else in the world mattered— no promises, no yesterdays, no tomorrow." He burnished a kiss along the delicate line of her jaw, curving away to nip at the lobe of her ear.

"Sweetheart," he whispered, "I'm not trying to get your sympathy this time, but I don't think I can stand up much longer. For a couple of reasons." He feathered kisses along each of her eyelids, disturbing the thick silken fringe of her lashes.

They made it as far as the doorway, and Dave leaned against the frame, gathering her to him once more. "Give me a minute, hmm?"

"Oh, Dave, does it hurt?" To Shea's chagrin, what she felt was not so much concern as impatience. She judged the distance to the bedroom and wondered if he'd consider her too forward if she dragged the mattress to where he stood.

"Just a muscle spasm," he grated. "It'll pass." His hands dropped to the top of her jeans, and he hooked his fingers there, gripping until his knuckles whitened. Moments passed, and then he managed a somewhat shamefaced grin as he began the task of undoing her fly.

Shea, torn between conflicting emotions, caught her breath as his touch seared her abdomen. "Are you sure?" she whispered, noticing that some of the color had drained from his face. She wanted him with a deep, sweet agony that all but robbed her of her sanity, but she could wait—maybe.

With excruciating slowness Dave lowered the zipper, revealing the narrow band of her underpants. Long before his hand slipped inside, Shea's breathing had all but ceased.

Arms dangling helplessly at her sides, she stood trembling before him, wondering how they were going to manage to get from doorway to bed. Would his leg cramp again if he tried to use it? None of her studies had prepared her for this sort of thing—the logistics of conducting a love affair without tripping over the first hurdle. What if his leg gave way and he fell? Which took precedence, sex or first aid?

"Dave," she began, her voice a wavering thread as she felt him slide his hands around to ease her jeans down over her hips. Clearing her throat, she tried again. "Dave, you might as well know that I don't take medicine—I mean pills."

The hands paused, and in the silence that followed, she fancied she could hear the thunder of his heartbeats. In a ragged voice he asked, "Not any kind of pills?"

Shea shook her head, sending her hair slithering about her neck. "Nope. Sorry. I just thought you should know."

"Or as they say in radio circles, over to you." Leaning his head back against the white painted doorframe, Dave closed his eyes. He might have known. God, what a time to put the skids on a man.

Miserably she murmured, "I wasn't expecting—I mean, I didn't think..."

Desire began to cool and resentment rushed in to fill the void. "Well, how was I to know you'd come barging into my house, criticizing everything in sight and wanting to make love to me?"

"How, indeed?" Dave mocked, his martyred tone making her want to strike out at something. Preferably him.

"Honey, I reckon it's time we had a long talk," Dave said, turning away from the door and limping across to the lavender chair.

Shea took advantage of the respite to zip her jeans and rebutton her smock. "Every time we talk we end up fighting," she reminded him.

"Is that so bad? Fighting with you is more fun than—" He'd been going to say, than making love to any other woman, but changed his mind. In her present mood she might not take it the right way.

On the surface, Shea decided, there might be some truth in what he'd said. Fighting with Dave was oddly exhilarating, now that she thought about it. Somehow it seemed to lack the destructive force that had torn her parents' lives apart.

"But you keep on not answering my questions," she countered in a weak defense against unconditional surrender. She dropped into the yellow chair across from where he sat.

"What questions are you talking about?"

"Well...questions." She toyed with the dried top of a red onion, systematically reducing it to shreds. "I've asked you lots of questions, and you never get around to answering any of them."

"Whenever I'm around you for any length of time, questions and answers don't seem all that important."

"Maybe not to you. I have to go a little more carefully," Shea pointed out. "If things go wrong, I've only myself to fall back on." Head bent over her task, she concentrated on removing a layer of crisp red skin from one of the decorative vegetables in the wooden bowl.

Dave continued to study her, unreasonably touched by the way her glossy brown hair curved under her delicate jaw as it fell away from her nape. No other woman in his whole life got to him the way she did. Either he found himself wanting to make love to every inch of her delectible body, or he felt compelled to protect her against anything and everything. Up to and including himself.

He sighed heavily. "Shea, you're not alone. You know you can count on me to look after you. And Jean. You're not without friends, you know."

Friends. *Friends?*

Shea lifted her face to stare at him. Was that what he was her *friend*? Was this the newest wrinkle in man-woman relationships? Living under the benevolent thumb of an elderly man whose idea of a liberated woman was one who was allowed to work outside the home until the children started coming, she'd learned a lot in theory, far less in actual practice.

But she knew one thing: it wasn't friendship that she wanted from David Pendleton, and if that was all he was offering, he could stuff it. She'd be better off the way she'd started out—alone.

"Look, honey, I realize you're pretty inexperienced about—"

"Inexperienced, but hardly ignorant. And what's that got to do with anything?" she demanded.

"I just thought—"

"Well, stop thinking about my problems—not that I have any—and start thinking about yours." Seeing his look of uncertainty, Shea felt the balance of power begin to shift in her favor. She took full advantage of it, jumping up to retrieve his shirt and sweater from her workbench.

She tossed them in his lap, gazing coolly down at the untidy thatch of his dark hair. "For instance, how am I going to get you home? My driveway looks like a parking lot already, and you're in no shape to drive."

"I could always spend the night," Dave hazarded, the beginning of a smile dancing in his eyes.

"If you think you can curl up in that rocking chair, you're welcome to try it. If not, I'll drive you home and dump you out, and we can sort out this mess of cars tomorrow."

"I can't ask you to do that," Dave began, his smile an obvious effort to tease her into submission.

Shea cut him off with an airy wave of one grimy hand. "Think nothing of it. What are friends for?"

Nine

———

Jean stopped by before Shea had even finished her breakfast the following morning. Shea answered the door to find her gazing out at the collection of vehicles lined up in the driveway, reaching all the way from cottage to highway. "Am I interrupting something, I hope?"

The expression on Jean's freckled face brought out a streak of mischief that Shea hadn't even been aware of possessing. "Only breakfast, but come in."

"I can come back later."

"Come on in. Don't stand on ceremony. You're almost like family by now."

Jean tossed her purse on the table, her avid eyes going from the closed bedroom door to the obvious breakfast preparations underway in the kitchen. In a heavy stage whisper she said, "Look, why don't I just slip out and call you later on this afternoon."

Shea took down another cup and filled it with freshly made coffee. "Sit down. I've got all the time in the world, and goodness knows, after last night I could use some relaxation." Eyes sparkling with laughter, she busied herself by slicing cheddar. "How about some cheese toast?"

"Some what?" Jean's attention was obviously not on food.

Still clutching the paring knife, Shea yawned widely, stretching her arms over her head. "I've got so much to tell you I don't know where to begin."

"At the beginning, you goose, and don't leave anything out. You're sure it's all right? I mean..." She nodded to the bedroom, where Shea had closed the door on her unmade bed.

After dropping Dave off at the hall the night before, she'd been far too keyed up to sleep. Instead she'd worked late into the night on the Leiberman order, roughing out six pairs of earrings and finishing one before finally surrendering to a few hours of restless dreams.

"I suppose you could say it started in Wilmington, but of course that wasn't the real beginning." Shea chose her words with care, knowing that she couldn't play the game too long. She wouldn't hurt her friend for the world but perhaps she owed Jean a little something for getting her off to such a rocky start with Dave.

"In Wilmington," Jean prompted. "I knew it. I could feel it in my bones."

"The weather was awful. I was soaked to the skin, and naturally, it hadn't occurred to me to take anything to change into. Of all times to look like a drowned rat, just when I wanted to make a good impression." She took a leisurely sip from her cup and dropped another slice of bread into the toaster. "Sure you won't have some toast? If you put the cheese on as soon as it pops up it almost melts."

"Shea," Jean said, showing signs of real stress. "'Wilmington'? 'Wet clothes'?"

"Oh, yes. Well, as I said, I was worried about the appearance I'd make. I mean, my whole future could hang on it, right? And there I was, my hair flopping around my neck like a wet mop, my sweater smelling the way wet wool always smells and my boots making a squishy noise every time I took a step. Men don't like women in squishy boots."

"So your boots were wet," Jean exclaimed impatiently. And then she grinned. "At least you didn't have to worry about a melting cast. I hope Dave thought to take along something for pain. His leg gives him fits whenever it rains and he's mean as the devil when he's hurting."

"'Dave'?" Shea repeated, all innocence.

"I keep telling him to wear a plastic bag over that thing when it rains, but you know my brother, bound and determined to go against any advice I give him."

"I seem to remember he wore a hunting sock," Shea murmured. "It smelled like wet wool, too."

"So enough of the wet wool. What happened next? First there was the accident, then you checked into a motel. Naturally I don't expect you to tell me *everything* that happened." She planted her elbows on the table, a look of avid curiosity on her face. "But what did happen, Shea?" she whispered. "Has he proposed yet? If I know Dave he won't want a big wedding, but maybe you could have something sort of semi-big and informal at the same time. You could wear a mantilla—you're entitled. You lived in Mexico long enough for that at least."

"Jean, slow up, will you?" Shea hadn't taken into account her friend's zeal for management. At this rate she'd be planning the honeymoon before her coffee got cold. "Jean," she said gently, intercepting another smug glance at the bedroom door. "He's not here. He didn't spend the night here, and we didn't share a room in Wilmington. Nothing happened."

Crestfallen, Jean stared at her. "Nothing?"

"Well . . . practically nothing," Shea amended, ashamed of herself for raising the hopes of someone who cared so much.

"But you're in love with him, aren't you? And he's in love with you. So what's the hold up? And what are both cars doing parked in your driveway so early in the morning if he didn't spend the night here?"

Shoving aside the breakfast she'd lost appetite for, Shea tried to explain what had happened. She could hardly tell Dave's sister that what she'd mistaken for love on his part at least was only a virulent strain of lust.

"You mean that hotheaded brother of mine talked the doctor into cutting him out of his cast a week early?"

"Actually, I think it was only five days early," Shea defended. "I was supposed to drive him to his appointment early next week." She attempted a grin. "Maybe he didn't like the way I drove."

"Or maybe..." Jean drawled with a maddening gleam of satisfaction. "Maybe he thought he could do a better job of courting you without it."

"I hardly think it was that," Shea retorted dryly, not bothering to add that he hadn't been doing badly even before.

"Oh, well, can't win 'em all. About your dog, Shea—I thought I had one lined up for you, but it didn't pan out."

A dog was the least of her worries at this point. "I don't suppose I could find one like Lady?"

"Later in the spring there might be a chance. That's when all the free kitten and puppy signs start sprouting like chickweed on every street corner. But Dave wants you to have one now."

"That's Dave's problem." Shea shrugged. "If I'm going to have a dog, it's going to be a case of mutual respect. Otherwise, what's the point?"

"Well, that eliminates my other prospect. You might have respected the one I thought I had lined up for you, but the owner came and claimed her. Only thing we've got at the shelter now is a pregnant bitch that looks like a cross between a rottweiler and a cow. You don't want her. Nasty disposition."

Over coffee they discussed Lee's braces, Joey's failing grades, Chan's newest scheme to win himself a sports car and Mike's choice of colleges. As if by unspoken agreement, they steered clear of any further mention of Dave.

Jean left with a reminder of her upcoming birthday celebration after a wistful look at the closed bedroom door.

Within the hour, Mike and Chan, driven by a friend, arrived to ferry Dave's two vehicles back home. After a short argument the older boy slid behind the wheel of the Porsche, revved the engine several times, then backed out cautiously onto the highway, followed by Chan in the Jeep.

End of an era, Shea thought, dismayed at the feeling of loss that assailed her. Now there'd be no reason to see Dave each day, no reason to spend a few hours with him, talking, arguing, laughing over inconsequential things, like Lady's inability to go down a set of stairs and Jean's inability to resist a homeless animal.

And her own inability to resist falling in love, even though she seemed fated to endure the same kind of relationship that had made her own childhood a living hell.

Closing the door of her cottage on the cold, damp wind that blew in off the ocean, she examined the single line of affection on the edge of her palm. *Last chance,* it seemed to say. *A single line, a single love, but if that doesn't work out, there's always your career line.*

Sometime after noon on the following day, Shea finished the last pair of earrings. The design was a simple one, a stylized oyster shell with a tiny sphere of silver representing a pearl. With no appointments to structure her days around, she felt oddly rootless.

Sleep had been elusive, and when it finally came, she dreamed of the bedroom she'd had as a child, hearing the music, seeing the pages and pages of compulsive doodling that had been her escape from the strife around her.

Wielding her torch later, she'd balled enough silver shot for all twelve earrings, hand-buffing the tiny drops to a pearllike luster. Lacking a grinder, she'd filed, then cupped the irregular ovals of flat silver, soldering on additional layers and burnishing the ruffled edges.

From now on she wouldn't be so quick to promise six of one style of anything, particularly earrings, which meant double the work. By the time she'd finished soldering the findings on the last pair, she was heartily sick of the repetitious work.

Several times during the day she thought she heard the sound of a familiar Jeep. She'd rush to the door, only to be disappointed. Once an elderly couple in hip boots drove past and parked just beyond her cottage. Miserably Shea watched from her back window as they climbed out of their yellow Jeep and waded out on the mud flats of Big Davis, carrying buckets and clam rakes.

The weak cold snap moderated, bringing with it a return to the more familiar warm, cloudy conditions. The ocean heaved restlessly, looking unusually swollen as a low-pressure cell combined with a full moon to bring higher than normal tides. Great for beachcombing, but even to Shea's inexperienced eyes, there were signs of erosion.

Tired of staying near the cottage in case Dave called or came by, she risked a soaking by going for a walk on the beach. And then, far from home, her hands filled with shells and bits of driftwood, she suddenly imagined her phone ringing off the hook and ran all the way back to an empty, silent house.

It was crazy. With a hundred things she needed to attend to, all she seemed capable of doing was moping over a man who couldn't be bothered to call and tell her he was all right. He claimed to be worried about her because she lived alone. Well, dammit, he lived alone, too, and she was worried about him!

Meanwhile there was Jean's birthday gift to make. And if she delivered the earrings to Hal Leiberman, she'd have enough money to buy herself something really special to wear to dinner Friday night.

With a substantial check in her purse the following day, Shea wandered from shop to shop, searching for just the right dress. Something flattering but not too expensive, seductive without being obvious about it. If she were smart, she'd drop Jean's gift off at her house, find an excuse to get out of the celebration dinner and spend the money on a drill press.

But, then, she'd never claimed to be brilliant. One thing she'd learned from reading all those palms: the subconscious knew a lot more than the conscious mind. Right now her subconscious was telling her to put everything she had on the line.

Dave dialed the number again and counted the rings. After twelve, he hung up, cursed feelingly and hoisted himself out of the deep leather chair. "Come on, old girl. Let's go see what the devil's going on out there, shall we? She might slam the door in my face, but I'd be willing to bet she won't be able to resist your bushy old snout."

He'd done his damnedest to stay away until he could sort things out, only it hadn't worked. She'd been on his mind constantly, coming between him and everything he tried to do, until he was more confused than ever. Finally he'd given in and tried to call her.

Since then he'd tried every hour on the hour. Either she wasn't home, or she wasn't answering her phone. For his own peace of mind he had to know which.

At least he had one worry lifted from his mind. Acting on a tip from a reliable source, DEA had moved their agent from Oak Island down to Shallotte Inlet. Of course, reliable sources had been known to be wrong, he reminded himself grimly as he gunned the Jeep and roared off down the driveway.

Her car was missing. Without so much as a single glance at the turbulent inlet that had occupied his mind for the past year and a half, Dave whipped the Jeep off the highway and came to a halt in front of the shabby green cottage. Kneading the stiffening muscles of his right calf, he draped one arm over the steering wheel and glared at the scrawny palms she'd planted beside her porch. The damned things had been dead when she'd bought them. Yet there they were, dutifully sending up new green shoots.

"I don't get it," he said to his canine companion, who gazed at him sympathetically. "Does she cast spells on every living creature she comes in contact with? Is she a witch? Are we all that gullible?"

Lady whined in response, and Dave reached out to ruffle her ears. "Talk about a charmed life…" He shook his head. "She buys a piece of junk from some con man she meets in a used-car lot, and the damned thing belches smoke and then runs like a sewing machine. She leases a cottage on a beach that's melting away under her very feet—'' Curling a fist, he brought it down on the steering wheel, a gesture of impotent frustration. ''I'm supposed to be some kind of an expert on beach erosion, but do you think she'd even ask my opinion? Hell, no! Dead palm trees miraculously come to life, worn-out cars purr like a kitten for her. Instead of cutting out, the damned inlet will probably start shoaling up just so she'll have a bigger yard.''

He restarted the engine and backed out onto the highway. A few minutes later he was pulling up in front of Jean's house. ''Lee!'' he called out to the thirteen-year-old who was shooting baskets on the front of the garage. ''Your mother home?''

''Nope.''

''Any idea when she'll be back?''

''Nope.''

''Is she at the animal shelter?''

''Nope.''

''Any plans to expand your vocabulary?''

''Nope.'' The boy grinned over his shoulder as the basketball rolled down the garage roof to land in a massive clump of pampas grass. ''Hairdresser,'' he supplied.

Hairdresser. The birthday dinner. At least he could be reasonably sure of seeing Shea tonight. She might not give him the time of day, but she wouldn't let Jean down. Meanwhile he'd better pick up some perfume or a scarf or something. And while he was at it, he could use a new shirt. It had been a while since he'd felt the urge to look presentable for an evening on the town. The fact that the occasion was his sister's birthday dinner must be a sign that he was settling down.

It was a sign, all right, he thought wryly. But it had nothing at all to do with Jean.

When the phone rang Shea was still in the bathtub. She'd shampooed her hair under the shower, then tossed in a generous supply of bath salts and settled down to soak the stains from her hands. The water had grown cool and her fingertips were beginning to look like seersucker, but at least they were clean.

Clutching the towel about her, she reached the phone on the sixth ring and panted a greeting into the receiver.

It was Dave. She'd known even before she heard his voice.

"Will you be ready in half an hour?" he asked, just as though nothing had changed between them since she used to drive him on his rounds.

"We're meeting at the restaurant, aren't we?" Surely he could hear the sound of her heart. Her breasts were trembling with every beat.

"I thought I'd collect you. It's not out of the way, and you might have trouble finding the place at night."

"You don't have to do that," she said breathlessly. "I can find it."

"No trouble," Dave tossed off carelessly. "Thirty minutes, then, all right?" And he hung up before she could think of an excuse.

Wool jersey in a soft shade of blue-violet wasn't too dressy, was it? Shea turned before the dresser mirror and tried to evaluate the effect of the surplice neckline and the bias cut of the swirling skirt.

At any rate, it was too late to worry about it now. She'd just heard the sound of Dave's car in her driveway. Dancing on one stockinged foot, she slipped on one of her new sling-back pumps and then wavered on the four-inch heel to pull on the other one. A spray of Fidgi, a touch of lipstick, and she was ready.

Her carefully contrived smile of greeting was already in place as she opened the door to his knock. It fell away, and her eyes widened in admiration. "You look...different," she told him.

"So do you," Dave said fervently, his gaze kindling to a palpable warmth as he took in the effect of the clinging blue fabric on her slight body. "So...do...you."

"Let me get—would you like to come inside? I just have to—" Oh, help! So much for her show of cool detachment. "I hope you realize that you're directly responsible for my incoherence," she said frankly.

"I am?" Dave drawled, stepping inside and closing the door behind him.

"It's the clothes, I think." Where had she put Jean's gift? Somewhere where she wouldn't forget to take it along. "Or maybe the cologne."

To her delight, he looked slightly discomfited. "Oh, well." He shrugged. "I'd ruined so many pairs of pants on account of that damned cast," he explained, dismissing the splendor of the flawlessly fitted pair of finely checked slacks, the shirt of ivory silk and a jacket the color of driftwood. "Lady sends her love."

"How is she?"

"I promised to bring her to visit. Would you like her to stay until you can find a dog of your own?"

Shea finally located the small gift-wrapped package in her good purse. She'd put it there, knowing she'd be using that one instead of her old straw clutch. "Jean's promised to find me a watchdog." She gave him a level look as he held the door for her. "Your idea, I understand. What's the matter, don't you think I can look after myself? Are you afraid my cottage might wash away and I won't wake up?"

"From the looks of that surf, that's not too farfetched."
He ushered her down the steps and out to where he'd parked
the Porsche. No Jeep tonight. Tonight he was courting in
earnest.

"So get me a lifeguard, instead," Shea suggested, holding on to his arm to empty the sand from her shoes before
she slid into his car.

"You already have one."

"You, I suppose," Shea said dryly. "You'd think someone had appointed you my guardian angel from the way
you've been acting. Did Jean put you up to it? Her moth-
ering instincts go too far sometimes."

This was the perfect opening, Dave thought as he drove
along the moonlit strip of highway toward the restaurant
where they were to meet Pete and Jean. Sooner or later he
was going to have to level with her about that letter, but
when it came right down to it, he found he didn't have the
nerve.

There was no sign of the Cummingses when they strolled
into the lobby. Dave nodded to the maître d', who greeted
him by name. He mentioned the reservations, and they were
immediately shown to a table set for two. The bedewed neck
of a champagne bottle protruded from a nearby silver ice
bucket, and in a crystal vase on the damask tablecloth a
spray of small pink orchids blushed in freckled splendor.

"There's been a mistake," Dave said quietly. "The reservations are for a party of four."

"Oh, no, sir. Mrs. Cummings called in again just an hour
ago to be sure everything was all arranged. Champagne,
oyster cocktails, broiled baby lobster with braised endive on
the side and whiskey pudding to follow."

"What, no whipped cream?" Shea murmured just loud
enough for Dave's ears. She might have known Jean would

get even with her for that stunt she'd pulled the other morning. This was supposed to be a punishment?

"Looks as if we've been set up," Dave said with a slow grin. He held her chair, and his hands lingered to brush over her shoulders.

"And I worked for hours to finish her birthday present in time." Shea did her best to look suitably disappointed, but her smile wouldn't be suppressed. Laughing navy eyes met sparkling gold ones. "I'm beginning to have a bit more sympathy for what you must have gone through all these years."

"Only this time the joke's on Jean. I've been racking my brains to figure out how I could dump Jean and Pete halfway through the evening and have you all to myself."

Shea's pulses leaped like the flame of the candle the waiter had just lit. "Have you?"

"Don't you want to know why?" Ignoring the interest of the wine steward, who was deftly uncorking the champagne, he reached across the intimate table to cover her hands with his.

Shea found it difficult to speak above a whisper. "You're going to ply me with food?"

"And champagne."

"And dessert," she murmured inanely. It was clear from the look in his eyes that the dessert he had in mind was not whiskey pudding.

By the time the ruins of a delicious dinner had been cleared away, the champagne bottle was empty. "There's dancing in the solarium," Dave supplied. "I think we'd better give it a shot before I drive you home." He didn't want any of his senses dulled by alcohol for what he had in mind.

"I don't think you're quite up to dancing, do you?"

"Try me," he murmured deeply, leading her out onto a closed-in deck where a handful of stars shone down through a glass roof. From somewhere amid a small jungle of shrubbery, a three-piece combo played a love song.

"What if we just hold each other up and sway to the music?" Dave turned to her, holding out his arms, and Shea walked into them and felt them close around her.

It was like coming home. She buried her face in the warmth of his throat, and they began a slow, rhythmic embrace as the strains of an alto sax drifted around them. Shea inhaled the enticing scent of his body, laced with a subtle new fragrance. She almost wished he'd left well enough alone. In his natural state of clean, healthy masculinity he was enough of a threat, without the added aphrodisiac of the understated cologne.

"Stars out," he whispered huskily, stirring her hair against her ear. "No doubt Madame Blueskies worked her magic on the weather."

"No doubt," Shea agreed in a dreamy murmur. His arms were around her, and in the dimly lit room, his hands were weaving a magic all their own as they played along her spine.

"Dancing's all right, but I can think of a better way to spend an evening." He stood perfectly still, holding her in a way that left her in no doubt about his meaning. "By the way," he said as he began to move again, "I like your new shoes."

"My new shoes?" Shea repeated blankly, still reeling from the effect he had on her. "Thank you. I didn't know you'd even noticed them."

"Oh, I noticed them, all right." The laughter that ran through his deep voice puzzled her still more. "I noticed them the minute we started dancing. We fit a whole lot better."

"Oh." Her face flamed as his hands dropped lower on her hips to press her against him.

"Let's get out of here," Dave said roughly.

Uncomfortable in an atmosphere laden with sexual tension, Shea was only too glad to comply. As he ushered her out into the crisp February evening, she searched for a safe topic of conversation.

Her cottage? She already knew his opinion of that. Her car? That would lead to another lecture, as well. Her work? At least they hadn't argued about that, but if she brought it up, no doubt he'd find some reason to criticize her judgment.

Even if she asked about Lady he'd use her interest to lead into a discussion on the reasons she needed a watchdog of her own. She simply couldn't risk an argument tonight. She was still giddy from the effects of the champagne...and Dave.

"You know," she blurted out, "you never did tell me what was in my grandfather's letter."

The tension inside the confines of the car suddenly soared to a new dimension. Shea, acutely sensitive to Dave's moods, could tell the precise moment the barriers went up.

His reluctance to discuss the matter only served to arouse her curiosity. "Are you too polite to tell me to mind my own business?" she taunted. "It's never stopped you before."

"Would it do any good?"

Unreasonably hurt—after all, she had brought it on herself—Shea stared at the craggy profile in the dim light from the instrument panel. "Probably not. For some reason, I keep thinking it is my business. Maybe because I carried that letter so many miles and then had to wait so long to deliver it."

Dave sighed heavily. "Oh, boy," he muttered under his breath. For a levelheaded scientist he'd been doing some

damned inefficient planning lately. Wasn't it Murphy's Law
that stated that whatever could go wrong, would go wrong?
Tonight was to be the grand seduction, either immediately
before or immediately following his carefully prepared pro-
posal of marriage. Hell, he'd even rehearsed the bent knee
just to be certain he could hold it without toppling over.

Only he'd forgotten to clear up the old business before
getting on with the new, and that just might be a major
mistake. No telling how she was going to take it. He'd been
a fool to think he could start off with this thing hanging over
his head.

"It's no big deal," he said in an offhand tone.

Shea waited. Arms crossed over her breasts, she waited
for something she knew in advance she wasn't going to like.

The low-swept car ate up the miles as the silence inside it
stretched out like spun glass. Shea felt her muscles tense in
an unconscious effort to steel herself. "Forget I asked," she
said when she could no longer stand it.

"No, dammit, I won't forget it," Dave snapped. He
slowed for her driveway and pulled up behind her own car.
Behind them moonlight danced on the restless surface of the
sea. "Your grandfather asked me to keep an eye on you,
that's all." He blurted out the statement and then waited for
the explosion that never came. "Well? What's so wrong
with that? I'd say it was a perfectly logical request, considering that you were all alone without a home or a job or
anyone to look after you until you got situated."

Still she didn't speak. Grinding his teeth, Dave told himself that she would probably make a big deal out of absolutely nothing. Hell, it had nothing to do with her as a
person. Anyone moving to a strange place would welcome
such an offer. Anyone except for a thin-skinned, cactus-
spined little mystic with a streak of independence a mile
wide.

"So you inherited me," Shea said in a surprisingly mild tone.

"You could put it that way, I suppose."

"The way my mother inherited me." She laughed, a forlorn little sound that twisted inside him like a knife. "Don't you think it's funny, a mother inheriting her own child? I do." Eyes wide in the dark interior of the car, Shea gazed through the windshield at the empty stretch of beach that surrounded her cottage. "Mother didn't. She hated it when Daddy walked out on us. She said if she'd had a grain of common sense she'd have known what he was up to and beat him to it."

"Honey, don't do this to yourself." Dave tried to gather her into his arms, but she pushed him away, huddling as far away as she could.

"So then, you see," she continued, as if she were explaining by rote an incident of historical record, "Granddad inherited me. And when he died, that meant someone else had to take me on. I called my father to tell him when—to tell him that . . ." She swallowed hard. "He was so afraid I was planning to move in with him that I almost laughed."

She tried it again, another soft, broken sound that faded before it even began. Dave knew better than to reach for her, no matter how badly he wanted to hold her and soothe away the pain.

"So now you've inherited me. And do you know what's so funny? All this time I thought I was really on my own. I'd been planning it for so long. Inez knew, but of course I couldn't tell Granddad. He was so weak that last month or two. It would have hurt his feelings. He'd have thought I didn't appreciate all he'd done for me, and I did. I really did."

For the first time she looked at him, but he couldn't be sure she was actually seeing him. "Dave, no one likes to be passed around like—like some hand-me-down coat."

"Shea, you know it's not like that," Dave said, his voice rough with gentleness.

"Do I?" she asked calmly.

It was that calmness that had him worried. He could have dealt with anger—at least, he thought he could. It was the hurt he couldn't take. The hurt that pinched her small features until her eyes looked like big bruises in a face gone pale as the moon.

It was the sight of her like this that flayed the very flesh from his bones. He'd have done anything in his power to have spared her this, only how could he have known she'd take it this way?

"Look, why don't I drive you over to Jean's and let you spend the night there, hmm?"

"Because I'm not capable of looking after myself, you mean?"

"No, dammit, because—well, just because."

"I'll go by Jean's tomorrow and drop off her present. Now I'd better get some sleep, because I still have three pendants and six brooches to do for Mr. Leiberman. Oh, and by the way," she added with a brittle animation that made him want to shake her, "I got my very first paycheck yesterday. It was enough to buy this dress, these shoes and a third of a drill press. Not too bad, huh?" She let herself out before he could come around and open the door for her.

With a feeling of helplessness unlike anything he'd ever experienced, Dave watched her pause on her porch to empty the sand from her shoes. One way or another he was going to have her. It might take a lifetime to convince her, but dammit, she was his!

Ten

_____

By midmorning Shea's headache was under control. Her guilt and embarrassment had grown to mammoth proportions. Regardless of the cost to her dignity, she knew she owed Dave an apology. It was hardly his fault that her grandfather had, to all intents and purposes, willed her to him. Under no obligation, he'd nevertheless done his best to comply with the old man's wishes.

Steeling herself, she dialed his number. "Dave? This is Shea." What did she say next? I'm sorry, I love you and goodbye?

"Good morning, Shea, how are you?"

At the sound of that grave, noncommittal voice Shea began to twist the cord around her wrist. "I'm fine, thanks. No, actually, I have a bit of a headache. I guess I'm not used to champagne." Excuses, excuses! She waited for his response, and when none was forthcoming she barged ahead.

"Look, about last night—all that silly business about, you know, inheriting me."

"Forget it, Shea." His sigh could have registered weariness or exasperation, she couldn't be sure. "I'm expecting a call," he went on, "but if you're going to be home later on, maybe I'll run out there."

"Sure, I'll probably be here." Feigning indifference, she told him goodbye and then set about retrieving her wrist from the tangle of cord.

All day long Shea examined the brief conversation for hidden meaning. Had he really wanted to come, or was it only that overgrown sense of responsibility she'd seen indicated in his palm? Was that all she was? An obligation? A duty?

No, she wouldn't believe that. Even Jean had said he was in love with her. Of course, knowing Jean's bias, Shea hadn't believed her for a minute. All the same, he was hardly indifferent, no matter how bored he'd sounded.

Did she dare trust her instincts instead of her intellect? Inez would have advised her to listen to her heart. Not that she had much choice in the matter, Shea reminded herself ruefully. She'd already jumped off the deep end, so it was a bit late for second thoughts.

For most of the day Shea made herself work on the Leiberman order. At four she gave up and took a leisurely bath. Dressed in white slacks and a yellow silk shirt, she spent more than an hour on her hair and nails.

The sun had just gone down, staining the beach a deep, coppery shade of rose, when Dave finally pulled into her yard. Lady was sitting sedately in the passenger seat beside him. "Sorry I'm late," he greeted her as Lady yipped a greeting of her own. "My editor called just as I was leaving, and we spent an hour going over the new batch of galleys. I didn't have time for Lady's walk, so how about it?

Shall we give her a turn on the beach?'' He lifted the shelty down to the ground, and Shea knelt to collect a wet kiss.

They followed after the old dog, not touching, hardly looking at each other. Shea was painfully conscious of the tall man strolling beside her, his features colored by the sunset. He was wearing a pair of ancient jeans and a faded cotton safari shirt that made his shoulders look broader than ever.

Lady's burst of energy was short-lived. Laughing, they watched from the top of a dune as she sniffed suspiciously at a head of spindrift and began backing away.

Dave mentioned the higher than normal tide. "I'd keep that life belt handy if I were you."

"But the water's nowhere near my cottage."

"Trusting little thing, aren't you?" He grinned lazily down at her, and Shea felt her resistance begin to erode, as if he were the tide and she were made of sand.

There were a dozen things she wanted to ask, but she couldn't remember a single one. By the time Lady walked stiffly up the dune again, she'd narrowed it down to a single question. Did he love her, or didn't he? He'd given her no indication, and she couldn't bring herself to ask.

Dave turned to follow the dog, and his shoulder brushed against Shea's. "Whoops—sorry, didn't mean to knock you down." He placed a steadying arm around her back, and every nerve in her body went into a tailspin.

"That's all right," Shea said, just as though his touch weren't burning her right through her shirt.

To Shea's chagrin he yawned. He obviously wasn't overcome by excitement at seeing her. She fought down an absurd desire to cry.

"Sorry about that," Dave murmured. They reached the Jeep, and he lifted the dog carefully into the seat again where she curled into a damp, sandy ball and tucked her nose under her bushy tail.

"Haven't had a lot of sleep lately. Last night was worse than usual." His glance was unreadable in the fast-fading light, and Shea's heart leaped with a crazy hope. Was that an admission of something?

Then it plummeted again as he continued to gaze at her silently. "I suppose you have to go," she said wistfully.

"Reckon I could spare a few minutes. Lady's settled for a while."

They were staring at each other intently, not touching, hardly even breathing. "You look sort of tired," Shea murmured. He looked tired and sleepy and wonderful, and she ached to stroke his hair back from his brow.

"Things on my mind. You look lovely tonight. Headache all gone?"

"'Headache'? Oh, yes—I mean, it's all gone. Would you like..."

The words trailed off. They were standing little more than a foot apart, their faces clearly visible now in the silver glow of the rising moon. A few ragged clouds raced by, casting iridescent shadows on the turbulent surf.

Afterward Shea was never certain who made the first move. Had he reached for her, or had she simply tumbled into his arms? It didn't matter. Nothing in the world mattered but this burning need to touch and be touched, to hold and be held. Shea's arms moved around him, and she buried her face in the damp, salty warmth of his throat.

"I missed you today," he said huskily.

"Me, too." She could feel his body's response, and she stood on tiptoe, craving a closer intimacy.

"You're not wearing your new shoes."

"For walking on the beach? Hardly," she whispered, laughing up at him.

With a groan he captured her laughter, raining kisses down on her lips, her eyes, her cheeks. He caught the lobe of her ear with his teeth and whispered wild and wonderful things to her. "God, you set me on fire! One look, one touch and—"

"Me, too," Shea blurted out, no longer able to maintain any semblance of control. "All I have to do is think about you and I'm lost." His firm, moist mouth settled once more over hers, the rhythmic dance of his tongue echoing the slow, achingly sweet movements of his hips.

Shea wondered how long her limbs could support her. If Dave felt as weak as she did, they'd both end up in a heap on the sand. A low murmur of delight escaped her as his hand wedged its way between them to capture her breast. Through a film of silk, her throbbing nipple grazed his palm. She clutched his hand to her, unable to bear the intensity of the pleasure.

"That single mattress of yours doesn't promise much comfort, but at least it's horizontal," Dave said with a shaky laugh. "Shall we got for it?"

"Hold on to me," Shea requested. "I don't want your weak leg giving out on us halfway to the porch."

"Heaven forbid!"

They made it to the house without coming to grief. Two shirts hit the floor before they'd even crossed the living room, and Dave held her away from him to gaze down at the slender perfection of her body. "You could be one of your own silver creations," he said gruffly. "So lovely. So incredibly lovely." Lowering his head, he kissed first one small, tilted breast, then the other. His tongue circled a tightly furled bud and he blew gently against her damp skin, and moaning, Shea clutched at his sides.

She swayed in his arms, her breath coming in small, quivering gasps. "Please," she panted. "I don't know if I can stand it."

Lifting his head, Dave smiled down at her, his eyes half-hidden in the shadows. "My sweet, lovely Shea. I haven't even told you yet—"

"Hush," Shea whispered, reaching up to press a finger to his lips. "One of us always talks out of turn, and this time I'm not having it."

Amused, Dave slipped his hands inside the seat of her slacks to feel the cool satiny softness of her buttocks. "You're not? What are you having, if you don't mind my asking."

"I'm having you. At least I hope I am."

Dave's hand came up to clasp her face. He gazed down at her features, at the short, straight nose that could register disdain more effectively than any nose he'd ever seen, at the silky dark lashes that shielded the most incredible eyes he'd ever encountered . . . at the lips that . . .

"I never even stood a chance, did I?" he murmured just before he lowered his face to hers.

Afraid of rushing her, he fought to control his own hunger. He wanted her so much he couldn't think of anything else, but he didn't dare risk ruining everything now. It had to be right for her— beautiful enough so that after tonight there'd be no more doubt in her mind.

He kissed her deeply, drowning in her singular sweetness, and they managed to cover the short distance to the bedroom. Any hope for control fled as the scent of her filled his nostrils, the feel of her filled his hands.

"Ah, love," he whispered hoarsely, "Let me show you how beautiful you are to me."

Quickly they shed the few clothes that remained between them. Her cool, soft body found the burning hardness of his, and holding him, she lowered herself to the mattress on the floor. "It's not very wide—I could spread the duvet on the floor."

"At least we don't have far to fall." Which was no lie. He'd already fallen as far as a man could.

With one hand Shea tugged the thick white comforter half onto the floor, and they tumbled sideways, laughing, holding on, trembling with the force of a need gone too long unfilled.

Propped on one arm, Dave leaned over her, gazing down at the play of moonlight over the subtle mounds and hollows of her body. Shea caught her breath on a shuddering sigh. The feel of his eyes on her was a palpable thing, incredibly stimulating. But she needed far more.

Lifting her hands to his chest, she brushed her fingers through the dark, flat curls, finding her tiny target with unerring accuracy. His immediate response excited her wildly. Continuing her explorations, she combed through the patches of rough hair on his chest and then let her hands wander down to his lean, satin-smooth hips, enchanted beyond belief by the way his body went from smooth to rough, to smooth....

Her fingers ventured over the rounded top of his thigh and lingered there, basking in the radiant heat from his aroused male body.

"Shea, I—"

With a whispered oath he broke off, lowering himself over her to separate her thighs with one of his. "My God, Shea, you're enough to drive a man crazy. So cool to touch, so unbelievably beautiful." His mouth moved feverishly over hers, his tongue darting through the barrier of her lips and then lifting again. His hand shaped to the soft rise of a breast and then moved on to the shallow depression of her waist, reaming the small pool that was her navel before sliding down to close over the shadowed thatch between her thighs.

At his intimate touch Shea gasped. Her eyes widened, then closed tightly. Fires that had been smoldering under the surface burst into raging flames, and she found herself clinging to the sharp edge of ecstasy as Dave's hand began a rhythmic dance. Half-wild, she clutched at his arm, stunned by the compelling forces he'd released.

"Tell me what pleases you." He drew a chain of shudderingly slow kisses down the sensitive tendon of her throat.

"I don't—" She broke off, wanting more, unable to express her deepest desire, unable to fight the sensations that were rising up like a tidal wave to engulf her.

Swiftly, as though divining her unspoken needs, Dave lifted himself onto his knees. Pausing only for a moment, he came down over her. At the first touch of the unfamiliar invasion Shea tried to draw back, and with a low groan Dave hesitated. She could feel him trembling above her, his control strained almost beyond belief.

Then his mouth covered hers, and Shea took him into her body, gasping as a hot, sweet wildness began to rocket through her whole being. Her eyes widened and then closed tightly, and she clung to him as the world grew smaller and then disappeared altogether.

For an endless fragment of time she could only hold on as the sweet tide of passion crested, then slowly subsided, leaving her weak and spent and totally helpless.

"My God," Dave breathed reverently when he could speak again. The words were compounded of wonder and reverence and love. "Are you all right, darling? Are you still with me?"

"I'm not sure," Shea returned, her voice a tremulous whisper. Never once relaxing his hold on her, Dave rolled onto his side. As his ragged breathing grew slower, the hands that caressed her began to relax.

Although deliciously drowsy, Shea was far too excited to give in to sleep. "I don't know if I happened to mention it, but I'm not really all that experienced. Next time... Well, the books I've read can't begin to compare with genuine hands-on experience."

When he made no reply she continued. "I've figured it all out, too, speaking of hands."

"Mmm?"

"Why we fight. It's your intellectual-type hand and my impulsive one. You think first. I act first. Actually, it's not all that big a problem once you understand what it is you're dealing with." She was chattering again.

"Dave?" Lifting her head from his shoulder, Shea peered at him. In the shadowy moonlight she could barely make out his features. "Dave, am I talking too much? I read an article once that said men didn't like—"

A soft snore issued from his throat, and she stared at him in disbelief. She'd just experienced the most wondrous event of her life and he was *sleeping*? "Isn't this when you're supposed to be telling me how much you love me?" she whispered plaintively.

Sighing, she lowered her head to his shoulder again. He'd said he hadn't been able to sleep. She'd had little enough sleep herself these past few nights. All the same, she could have used a little reassurance. "I love you, you fearful wonderful wretch, and if you think I'm going to let you go now you're crazy!" she murmured threateningly.

It seemed only moments later when Shea awoke. Disoriented, she watched the flash of red light that circled her room, reflecting on everything in its path. The heavy weight on her shoulder corresponded to the heavy lethargy that seemed to have invaded her limbs. She turned to stare down at the sleeping man beside her. It had really happened, then. She hadn't just dreamed it all.

Sighing, she turned back to watch the relentless light show. She'd heard of hearing bells, of feeling the earth move—but flashing red lights?

The lights were coming from outside the house. As reality began to seep in, replacing her fantasy, Shea lifted her head to listen. Was that the sound of voices, or only the sound of the surf?

"Dave? Dave, wake up," she whispered. She took his shoulder. "There's something going on out there."

Muttering something unintelligible, Dave reached for her and drew her down on top of him, pressing her face into his throat. "There's something going on in here that's even better," he said drowsily.

From outside came the definite sound of voices, accompanied by Lady's agitated barking. Instantly alert, Dave sat up, moving Shea aside. Reaching across her, he grabbed his pants and got to his feet. "Stay put. I'll check it out."

Shea had no intention of staying put, not with all those emergency lights flashing around her house, not with Lady out there barking her silly old head off. "I'm coming with you," she whispered urgently. "If we're washing away, we'll wash together."

Dave tugged at his zipper, looking down at the small figure thrashing around in a tangle of bedclothes in search of her pants. A surge of fierce possessiveness welled inside him. "You're not going out there."

"Of course I'm—" She grunted, shoving a foot in the tangled leg of her pants. "I'm going with you. I'm not about to let you go out there alone! Besides, if something's going on outside my house, I'm going to be in on it. Where are my shoes? Have you seen my shoes?"

"Forget your shoes? You're not setting one foot outside this house until I tell you it's safe, is that clear?"

Shea stared at him in openmouthed disbelief. "Are you telling me—" she began, when he cut her off.

"Read my palm," he growled, holding the flat of his hand in front of her stunned face. "You're staying right here. You can be as independent as you want to be some other time, but right now you're going to stay inside if I have to hog-tie you with your own shirt."

In took a while for the words to register. By this time, Dave was out the door, fastening his belt and buttoning his shirt as he went. Shea stared at him, anger and indignation in every line of her body. By the time she'd located her shoes and her shirt the lights had stopped flashing, leaving the bedroom curiously still.

Grimly she made her way through the dark house, expecting to hear the sound of waves slapping against her walls at any moment. She didn't know where all the light had come from, and until she knew Dave was safe she didn't care. If he'd gone and got himself hurt she'd kill him!

Good Lord, the circus had hit town!

"Hi, there, Shea. Dave said he thought you'd already turned in." Jean ambled up to meet her, leading a pathetic looking animal on a makeshift leash. "Look what I brought you."

"Jean? What's going on out here? Who are all these people?" Shea stared at the assortment of vehicles, recognizing a yellow truck from the Department of Transportation and a car with a Coast Guard emblem on the door. "Isn't that Chan's VW? Is he here, too?"

"I made him drive me in case I had trouble with the Duchess." Jean indicated the cringing, slat-thin mutt, who seemed to be molting, from the looks of her wiry brindle coat. "If you don't like the name feel free to change it. She' a bit down on her luck at the moment, but she'll clean up real good. Half-starved, poor critter, but basically healthy."

"Jean, would you mind telling me who all those people are and what they're doing here? You didn't need an official escort just to bring me a dog, did you?"

Jean leaned against the Jeep. Lady growled a warning, and the Duchess groveled her way between Shea's firmly planted feet, nearly knocking her over in the process.

"See there? Knows her mistress already," Jean observed smugly.

Shea raked a hand through her hair and tried once more. "Nobody answers questions around here, did you know that? Is it just my imagination? Am I not getting through?" She raised her voice, underlining each word for emphasis. "Jean, *who are all these people in my front yard*?"

"Well, there's Chan, of course. I told you that, and you knew Dave was here. What's he doing here, anyway? Don't tell me he was going to let you borrow Lady."

At the sound of her name Lady began barking again. Dave, who'd been talking to some strange man in a dark sedan, sauntered over, followed closely by Chan. Duchess, having slunk to the limits of her leash, buried her nose between her paws and gazed up with mournful eyes, obviously resigned to whatever new blow fate had in store for her.

"Ma, can I go home with Uncle Dave and listen in on ham radio?"

"No," Jean said flatly.

"Would someone please tell me what's going on around here?" Shea pleaded.

Ignoring her, Chan turned to Dave. "I heard that guy say something about a bust going down near Cork Creek Landing. Where's that? Who is the guy? Are you mixed up with the feds?" A grin spread over his broad face. "Hey, that's it, isn't it? Man, that's really neat! My own uncle, an undercover—"

"Jean, if you value the health of your middle son you'll get him out of here."

"Why? I'd like to know what's going on, too, now that you mention it."

"Anything you need to know I'll tell you tomorrow," Dave said tersely.

"Is that a promise?" Jean drawled, her eyes going from Dave to Shea and back again.

Helplessly, Shea followed the exchange. Perhaps she'd suddenly become invisible. It might explain why no one paid any attention to her questions. She opened her mouth to remind them of her presence and closed it again. Why bother?

Dave eyed the grizzled mongrel who seemed intent on hiding between Shea's small moccasins. "Jean, you're not serious about saddling Shea with this flea-ridden specimen, are you?"

Shea's toes tucked possessively under Duchess's bony sides. Invisible or not, there was a limit to her patience. "Watch what you say about my dog. And would you *please* tell me what's going on out there?" She jabbed a forefinger toward the broken end of the pavement, where several men still stood milling around an assortment of vehicles.

There was a moment of utter silence, and then Jean said, "Don't look at me. I only came to deliver the Duchess."

"Geez, Shea, a big chunk of beach got washed out, and then there was this—"

"And don't listen to him, either. He watches too much television. Come on, Chandler, drive me home. You've got school tomorrow, don't forget."

Shea waited for Dave to speak. He was the one she needed to hear from. He moved to her side and placed a hand on her shoulder, and instantly the Duchess lifted her head to growl a warning.

"Oh, good Lord, what next?" he burst out. "I haven't slept for three nights—"

"Sure you have," Shea reminded him, arms crossed over her breasts. "Matter of fact, you snore."

"The hell I—" His shoulders fell, and he looked at her uncertainly. "Do I?"

She had to laugh. "Dave, would you please tell me what's going on around here? The trucks and all that business about feds and . . ."

"Believe me, this wasn't the way I envisioned things when I set out to propose to you tonight."

Shea's jaw fell. Beyond her driveway the DOT truck backed around and left, followed by the dark sedan. Chan tooted the first bar of the Confederate anthem on his horn, and Jean called to remind Shea that her new dog would need a license as soon as possible.

After what seemed an eternity they were alone again. The stillness was broken only by the muffled roar of the surf and the occasional cry of a night bird. Lady, evidently no longer feeling threatened, was draped over the passenger seat of the Jeep, her head angled so that she could keep a wary eye on the Duchess. Dave leaned his hips against the cool metal and opened his arms, and stepping over her brand new watchdog, Shea walked into them.

"I thought you'd never ask," she murmured, her voice brimming with resigned laughter.

"I haven't . . . yet." Dave buried his face in her hair, inhaling the sweet, clean scent of her. What timing! He'd planned on proposing to her first, but at the sight of her, at he very first touch, all his plans had flown out the window. Then he'd committed the unpardonable sin of falling asleep, his declaration still undeclared, and awakened to find all hell had broken loose.

"I didn't mean—" Shea hesitated. "I only meant I thought you'd never ask me into your arms. It was a silly— oh, Dave," she wailed helplessly, "do you suppose I'll ever learn not to chatter like a magpie?"

"Maybe with a little help you could lick the habit," he murmured deeply just as his lips brushed over hers.

Shea's arms went up around his shoulders and she was lost once more, all thought of Jean and strangers in dark sedans and shivering mongrels forgotten as she gave herself up to the sheer heaven of his kiss.

A long time later she was roused by the feel of a cold nose nudging her ankle. Resting her head on Dave's chest, she reached down a hand and felt for the knobby head of her protector. "Is anyone ever going to answer my questions?" She sighed plaintively.

"I have a question of my own, but go ahead, ladies first."

At the sound of her name Lady perked up. Her whine alerted the Duchess, who growled a warning, which in turn elicited a snarl from Dave's dog.

"Oh, great balls of fire," Dave cried, lurching away from the hood of the Jeep. "Could we go inside and leave these two to fight their own battles? They'd better learn to get along, and damned fast, because if I have my way, they're going to be sharing a roof before much longer."

With one dog waiting in the car and one standing guard on the porch, Dave closed the door firmly behind them. "Look, before anything else happens, could I please just ask you one question? Will you marry me?" There was a note of desperation in his voice.

"Oh, yes, please." All but melting with love for him, Shea nevertheless felt it necessary to voice a reservation. "We're probably going to fight a lot, you know."

"For the first fifty years, at least," Dave agreed, his eyes suspiciously bright in the stream of moonlight that spilled into the room. "Does it matter?"

Trembling, Shea could barely hear her own words over the sound of her heart. "Not if you love me," she whispered, and he caught her to him, holding her as if he'd never let her go.

"Love you! God, haven't I told you yet how much—" Breaking off, he swore softly. "No, I guess I haven't. You see?" He grinned crookedly down at her. "That's what happens to me whenever I get close to you. My brain turns into sawdust and I trip over my own feet."

He was planting soft kisses on her eyes, her nose, her temple. Just before his lips closed over hers Shea slipped her hand up to hold him away. "Do you suppose the effect will last? It might sort of even the odds if I didn't have to go up against one of you cool intellectual types."

His arms tightened until she could scarcely breathe. "Does this feel like a cool intellectual body you're up against? I promise you, precious, you can be as impulsive and as independent as you want to be. I love the woman you are, and I'm not about to try to change you."

Shea felt a slither of silk as her shirt fell to the floor. Her hands dropped to the buttons on his chest and she fumbled in the darkness. "You still owe me some answers, you know."

"Such as?" His deft fingers set to work on the fastening of her slacks, a task made doubly difficult because neither of them was willing to release the other.

"Such as," Shea managed breathlessly as she stepped out of her pants and kicked them aside, "my dog or yours? My house or yours? I can't turn the Duchess away—she needs a home. And even though the cottage is sort of drafty and the roof leaks, I'm really fond of my palm trees."

Dave laughed, and the deep rumble transmitted itself to Shea's body, setting off a series of delicious reverberations. "We'll have plenty of room for two dogs and a couple of palm trees, love. But for safety's sake, humor me and get rid of that car, will you? If you won't let me help you pick out a replacement, at least let one of Jean's boys advise you."

"We'll see," Shea murmured diplomatically. Her car was the last thing on her mind at the moment.

"You can have any room in the house you want for a workshop, sweetheart. There's plenty of space for you, your watchdog and your silverworking gear, too."

Running her hands inside the waist of his pants, Shea eased the slacks down over his hips as if she'd been doing it all her life. "Speaking of silver," she murmured, "we're going to have a double dose of heirloom silver. Maybe we'd better see what we can do to line up a few heirs."

From the porch outside came a soft thump as the Duchess settled down for a long wait.

Silhouette Desire

COMING NEXT MONTH

THE FIRE OF SPRING
Elizabeth Lowell

Logan didn't believe in love, he believed in revenge. When he won Dawn Sheridan's ranch in a poker game he should have been satisfied, but he wasn't. Dawn was the perfect target for his anger. Yet he found that in hurting her, he came away wounded.

THE SANDCASTLE MAN
Nicole Monet

Sharon wanted Michael's child but he was gone and all she could cherish were empty dreams. Until she met Rob Barnes. Together they shared a dream, with no promises or commitments made. But now it was time to reach past the fantasy to reality waiting just beyond.

LOGICAL CHOICE
Amanda Lee

Dressed in a clown costume Diana flirted with Blake Hamilton. She knew it was dangerous and hoped that he wouldn't learn her true identity. But Blake was determined to find out more about the woman beneath the greasepaint . . .

COMING NEXT MONTH

CONFESS TO APOLLO
Suzanne Carey

Alex combined the best of the old and the new, and it was clear that he wanted Zoe. But to be Alex's woman would mean making peace with her grandmother who had dominated her childhood. Could their love give her the courage to face the past and open the way to the future?

SPLIT IMAGES
Naomi Horton

Cassidy had interviewed celebrities on her talk show but no one had irritated her the way Logan Wilde had. The author of the hottest sex guide had virtually seduced her on live television. And then he had the audacity to ask her out on a date.

UNFINISHED RHAPSODY
Gina Caimi

Jason was Lauren's guardian. He had been her world, but he seemed determined to mould her to fit his own vision. So Lauren left. Four years later she returned, an acclaimed concert pianist. But the moment she looked into Jason's eyes she knew her attempts to free herself of him had failed.

Silhouette Desire Romances

TAKE 4
THRILLING SILHOUETTE
DESIRE ROMANCES
ABSOLUTELY FREE

Experience all the excitement, passion and pure joy of love. Discover fascinating stories brought to you by Silhouette's top selling authors. At last an opportunity for you to become a regular reader of Silhouette Desire. You can enjoy 6 superb new titles every month from Silhouette Reader Service, with a whole range of special benefits, a free monthly Newsletter packed with recipes, competitions and exclusive book offers. Plus information on the top Silhouette authors, a monthly guide to the stars and extra bargain offers.

An Introductory FREE GIFT for YOU.
Turn over the page for details.

As a special introduction we will send you **FOUR**
specially selected Silhouette Desire romances
— yours to keep **FREE** — when you complete
and return this coupon to us.

At the same time, because we believe that you will be so thrilled
with these novels, we will reserve a subscription to Silhouette
Reader Service for you. Every month you will receive 6 of the very
latest novels by leading romantic fiction authors, delivered direct to
your door.

Postage and packing is always completely
free. There is no obligation or commitment —
you can cancel your subscription at any time.

It's so easy. Send no money now. Simply fill in and post
the coupon today to:-

SILHOUETTE READER SERVICE, FREEPOST,
P.O. Box 236 Croydon, SURREY CR9 9EL

Please note: READERS IN SOUTH AFRICA to write to:-

Independent Book Services P.T.Y.,
Postbag X3010, Randburg 2125, S. Africa

- -

FREE BOOKS CERTIFICATE

To: Silhouette Reader Service, FREEPOST, PO Box 236,
Croydon, Surrey CR9 9EL

Please send me, Free and without obligation, four specially selected Silhouette Desire Romances and reserve a
Reader Service Subscription for me. If I decide to subscribe, I shall, from the beginning of the month following my
free parcel of books, receive six books each month for £5.94, post and packing free. If I decide not to subscribe I
shall write to you within 10 days. The free books are mine to keep in any case. I understand that I may cancel my
subscription at any time simply by writing to you. I am over 18 years of age.
Please write in BLOCK CAPITALS.

Name _____

Address _____

_____

_____ Postcode _____

SEND NO MONEY — TAKE NO RISKS
*Remember postcodes speed delivery. Offer applies in U.K. only
and is not valid to present subscribers. Silhouette reserve the right
to exercise discretion in granting membership. If price changes
are necessary you will be notified.
Offer limited to one per household. Offer expires July 31st
1986.*

EP18SD